To Emiko,

hugs.

Mary Ban

April

2014.

BOOK 1

The Ditch Dog

BOOK 2

The Hedge Cat

Mary Barr

iUniverse, Inc.
New York   Bloomington

Book 1 - The Ditch Dog/Book 2 - The Hedge Cat

iUniverse books may be ordered through booksellers or by contacting:

iUniverse
1663 Liberty Drive
Bloomington, IN 47403
www.iuniverse.com
1-800-Authors (1-800-288-4677)

ISBN: 978-1-4401-5558-1 (pbk)
ISBN: 978-1-4401-5560-4 (cloth)
ISBN: 978-1-4401-5559-8 (ebk)

Printed in the United States of America

iUniverse rev. date: 9/25/2009

BOOK 1
The Ditch Dog

Dedication

The Ditch Dog is dedicated to my best friend, mentor, and the one special person who inspired me more than any other: a woman who taught me love conquers all and who had an unyielding belief that I could achieve anything and become anyone I chose.

The place you hold in my heart will forever be yours. Mothers are very special; you have only one and I miss mine every day.

I dedicate this book to my mother, Peggy Ethel Richardson, who sadly passed away on

December 13, 2002.

Like Ditto, the Ditch Dog, you are truly a free spirit...

Contents

CHAPTER ONE
Ditto and the Invisible Dog

It was a warm, fuzzy, August morning. Tiny white puffy clouds floated lazily across an azure sky. A gentle breeze tickled the air, bringing with it autumn's early morning smells. The bees hummed softly, while the early birds created a chorus of birdsong as they celebrated the beginning of another new and wonderful day.

Ditto was a ditch dog, a scruffy, happy ditch dog. His shaggy coat was once white with patches of dark brown but now appeared a matted gray with large patches of dirty black. Ditto had large, gentle, light brown eyes, floppy ears, and a tail that usually wagged approval, whether or not there was any approval that needed wagging about; Ditto was a happy dog.

Ditto slept neatly curled up in one of his favorite ditches. All around him, the grass grew green and lush beside the lazy country lane. He slept securely under a gentle weeping willow tree; its branches long, while the lazy breeze ruffled the leaves as they tickled his nose. Ditto first opened one eye, then the other as slowly the early morning noises intruded on his sleep, awakening him gently as they welcomed him to the new day.

"Wake up, Ditto! The sun's already over the tall old pine tree,"

Swirly Squirrel said, hanging from the longest branch of the willow tree. Reaching down, Swirly tickled Ditto's nose with a fresh, long stem of grass. Ditto could hear Swirly's high-pitched giggle followed by the sound of the tiny red squirrel scurrying high into the branches the moment he stirred. Ditto stretched, just as he'd been taught as a puppy—he pulled his body out as far as it would go so he could become the longest dog he could possibly be. He yawned, wagged his tail at nothing, and sat down again, surveying the morning.

It was a good day, Ditto thought, strolling slowly over to the little stream in the meadow. He lapped at the cool water, quenching his early morning thirst. Then he spied a butterfly opening and closing its large wings on a small rock nearby. Ditto loved chasing butterflies! It was one of his favorite things in the whole world! He thought about it all day long; he even dreamed about it at night.

Just then, Ditto's tail began wagging wildly with excitement. He yapped loudly before jumping around in circles. The butterfly did not move. It just sat opening and closing its wings, teasing Ditto, until slowly it began to fly. Ditto was so excited he completely forgot he was on one side of the stream while the butterfly was on the other. He jumped high into the air as he leaped eagerly toward the butterfly. It was such a pretty, colorful butterfly, and Ditto always enjoyed an early morning game of chase. Ditto never thought he'd actually catch a butterfly, but he was sure going to try. The fun was in the chase, anyway.

Ditto landed—*splash!*—in the middle of the chilly stream. The water quickly soaked his belly, as he immediately remembered the stream between himself and the butterfly. After briefly hovering over Ditto, the beautiful butterfly slowly flew off. Ditto stayed exactly where he was, gazing after it and wishing he, too, could fly so gracefully through the air. The butterfly circled over Ditto several times, teasing him just a little more. Each time Ditto leaped high into the air, but always the butterfly remained just out of reach. Soon, the butterfly tired of the early morning game and flew off to do whatever butterflies do every day when they're not being chased by ditch dogs.

As he stood on the grassy bank, Ditto shook himself again before rolling long and deeply in the grass. This time, he very nearly had that butterfly, he thought, his tail wagging madly. Very nearly, but not quite. Again Ditto rolled in the grass, nibbling on a few choice pieces before drinking a little more of the cool stream water.

Ditto always closed his eyes when he drank, but today for just a second he opened one eye. As he looked into the clear water of the stream, he saw another dog. Frightened, Ditto immediately leaped backward, cowering low in the long grass. The dog in the water looked horribly unkempt; he was a scruffy-looking dog, maybe not unlike himself. However, the thing that scared Ditto most was how close the dog was to him, almost nose to nose—and he hadn't even known he was there! Ditto liked nearly all dogs, but he had never seen this dog before. It scared him.

Ditto laid flat against the grass as slowly he looked around to see where the dog was hiding. He couldn't see it anywhere! Maybe the other dog felt just as scared. Maybe it would like to play, Ditto thought, as slowly he wagged his tail, not a fast wag but just a little wag on the end. Ditto waited patiently in the grass for the other dog to appear. He waited and waited; he watched and waited. More time passed, but still he couldn't see the dog anywhere.

CHAPTER TWO
Ditto Visits the Village

Ditto wasn't sure he wanted to stay and play with a dog he couldn't see. He decided an invisible dog wouldn't be much fun, anyway. If it was as shy as Ditto thought it was, what sort of friendship could they have? Maybe the dog was already playing hide and seek with Ditto! He loved hide and seek, but as he looked around, he couldn't see the other dog anywhere. Maybe it has already found a good hiding place!

Ditto was not a shy dog. He was a fun, happy kind of dog who enjoyed meeting new people and dogs. He loved learning new things and seeing the world. The sun had moved higher in the sky now, and Ditto knew he had places to go and people and dogs to see. He wasn't even sure the other dog wanted to play, and if it wouldn't even show itself, Ditto knew it wouldn't be much fun.

He lingered just a few minutes longer, waiting and watching, until reluctantly he realized the other dog really didn't want to play after all. Ditto shook himself off again and headed toward the back meadow. He knew it was the safest way to travel; the grass was taller there, perfect for hiding, and if the dogcatcher was searching for him, he wouldn't be able to easily spot him. Ditto was nearly into the long grass when he heard a voice.

"Ditto, come and play! It's a great day, and Betty and I are thinking of playing chase out in the meadow. Do stay and join us?" It was the deep, raspy voice of Badley Badger; he bounded toward Ditto. Betty Badger was one of the sweetest animals Ditto knew; she cared about everyone. You could rely on her completely, no questions asked. Ditto had always thought the Badger family very handsome with their striking black stripes over both eyes and clean white stripe down the center. He found their flat, chubby bodies quite unique— rather funny and sort of cuddly all at the same time; and they sure could run fast.

"No thanks, Badley and Betty. I'm off to see my friends in the village. They always bring me treats." Ditto politely answered the Badgers.

"Well, now, you be wary of them humans. Very unpredictable creatures all those nice little doggies they keep on a piece of rope!" Badley warned, before Betty interrupted him.

"Oh, Badley, leave Ditto alone! He has to decide on his own just whom he wants as his friends. You always said choice was a good thing, remember?" she added, playfully nudging Badley.

"I know I said that, dearest, but I think one day Ditto and I should race in and free all those poor little doggies and bring them home with us!"

"I think they stay because they want to, Badley", Ditto said. "I know the only reason they're on the end of a rope is because of the nasty dogcatcher who roams around." Ditto said, still eager to leave.

"Oh, Ditto, he would love to catch you. Do be careful! Stay in the ditches and shadows," Betty called, the concern evident in her voice. Ditto smiled, knowing they were both his good friends.

"Okay, Betty. I promise to be careful. Have fun playing chase," Ditto called over his shoulder.

Ditto turned, tail wagging, and headed in the direction of the village. It was one of his special places in the whole world and always so much fun. Ditto ran swiftly along the edge of the meadows, staying hidden in the tall grass. Ditto loved the feeling of the long grass as it brushed against his coat and face. As he ran, the cool breeze stung his eyes, but he didn't care. He loved the feeling of freedom more than anything. So, with his ears flapping against his head and his tongue hanging out, Ditto continued running just as fast as he could. He always felt the same excitement as he headed toward the village. He had many friends there, and it was fun seeing them and their dogs as they walked the village common.

As he neared the village, he headed for the safety of the ditch. For as much fun as visits to the village were, Ditto constantly remembered the dogcatcher and his fondness for catching stray dogs. Ditto knew he was definitely a stray dog.

Sometime later, Ditto was safely in the big ditch at the far end of the common under a very large oak tree, its leaves already beginning to turn golden as it notified the world autumn was fast approaching. The first friend to greet Ditto was Bruce, an Old English Sheepdog. Bruce's long, shaggy coat was black at the back, while the front was very white and fell over his eyes like the fringe on a long woolen scarf. Ditto knew Bruce was a happy, loved dog, who was very content and always beautifully groomed. Today, Bruce proudly wore a new brown dog harness with a matching leash, held firmly by ten-year-old Rex, whose mother followed close behind. The moment Bruce saw Ditto, he gently guided Rex toward the ditch.

"Hello, ditch dog," Bruce said in his deep, slow, voice.

"Hello," echoed Rex in his high-pitched young boy's voice, brushing a stray red curl from his large brown eyes. Rex wore an old, blue check shirt and long faded red jeans; they appeared much too large for him as they hung down around his hips. Young Rex held them up with one hand while holding Bruce's leash firmly in the other.

"Look, ditch dog—I'm wearing my brand new dog harness. It's very comfortable, and I don't choke if Rex pulls too hard. Do you like it?" Bruce asked, holding his head high and turning proudly around several times. His shaggy coat shone in the sunlight as he peered through his long fringe at Ditto.

"Yes, Bruce, it's very smart," Ditto, answered, even though most of the harness was completely hidden under Bruce's long shaggy coat.

"We got it especially for Bruce's birthday! He's a loved dog, not like you, ditch dog! You're very scruffy!" Rex added honesty, but kindly.

"Yes, but I'm free, and I can do whatever I want, whenever I want," Ditto added, defending himself as he always did.

"Rex, didn't you have something for the dirty ditch dog?" Rex's mother said in a kind voice.

"No, Mummy. I left it at home. I have some bread for the ducks. Would you like some, ditch dog?" Rex asked embarrassed as he turned one corner of his lip down and softly kicked the ground.

"You forget everything, Rex," added Bruce, lazily shaking his thick coat.

"No, it's okay. I wouldn't want to take the ducks' lunch from them," Ditto reluctantly answered, seeing Rex's embarrassment as his stomach growled.

"You're a good, kind, considerate ditch dog. I think you should come home with us. We can clean you up and love you. We'd be your very own family," Rex said, excited now.

"Thank you, but I like being a ditch dog. I have my freedom; so you see I can do whatever I like. But thank you again for the offer, Rex," Ditto added, his tail wagging madly as he spoke.

'Oh, you're a silly ditch dog! Don't you know you're not a real dog unless you have someone who loves you?" said Bruce in his slow, gruff voice.

"I have many friends and I know they all like me a lot. Does that count?" Ditto asked,

"I'll have to think about it and tell you next time we see you. Bye, ditch dog," said Bruce and Rex as they turned and walked away. After they left, Ditto quickly checked for the dogcatcher before backing further into the shadows.

Moments later, Ditto heard the loud voices of the Rawlinson kids as they bounded into view. Blackie was a tall, excitable Standard Poodle. Constantly in motion, he continually yapped and barked loudly. Today, as usual, he wore a large red collar as he dragged young Janet Rawlinson in Ditto's direction. Following closely behind the scruffy pair came the two older Rawlinson boys, Billy and Donny, while behind them scampered the two younger boys, Ronny and Willy. They were dirty, noisy kids; and Ditto noticed as usual, they ran everywhere and had no control over Blackie whatsoever. As they came toward Ditto, he could hear young Ronny and Willy arguing loudly over who had won the most marbles at school yesterday.

Janet was the only girl and Ditto secretly thought her very pretty, but like her brothers she always looked as though she'd been rolling around in the dirt and dust. Her jeans were worn and scruffy, her faded pink T-shirt was covered in grass stains; today Ditto noticed several small holes had appeared. Ditto particularly liked her hair. It was a soft, light golden brown and curled up at the ends just below her shoulders. Ditto's favorite time was when she wore it in a ponytail, and it swung back and forth as she ran. Today, her hair was again dusty and had leaves and grass in it, just like the boys' hair. Janet had the whitest teeth Ditto had ever seen, and the bluest eyes. Yes, Ditto thought, she was a pretty girl. Ditto often wondered just how good-looking the Rawlinson children would be, if they'd occasionally change their clothes and took a bath.

"Hi, ditch dog!" the five children said in unison as Blackie leaped toward Ditto, barking wildly as his tall front legs left the ground. Ditto knew Janet must be a very strong girl to restrain him at all; he barked and yapped constantly and never stopped moving, even when he spoke. Even though Blackie was a tall, handsome Standard Poodle, unlike most poodles he had never been seen the groomer. Like the Rawlinson kids, Blackie was always rather dirty, with twigs and grass hidden in his matted coat. However, someone was clearly trimming his tail, as the end stayed perfectly shaped in a large round ball. Ditto knew Blackie was very proud of his tail.

"Ditch dog, you should find a home! Yes, that's what you need, a home. Then you could be a dog who someone loves! Guess what we did today—it was so much fun! Oh yes it was! Guess, guess, guess!" Blackie barked. He continued to move madly to and fro, pulling wildly on his leash and dragging Janet two more feet toward Ditto. As hard as she tried, she was unable to hold Blackie back.

"Okay, just what did you do today, Blackie?" Ditto politely asked the excitable pooch.

"We played Frisbee! Oh yes, that's what we did, yes it was! It was fun, oh yes, so much fun, ditch dog!" Blackie said talking as fast as he moved, all the while jumping and barking madly.

Willy and Ronny stopped arguing and added, "If you were a real dog and not a scruffy ditch dog, you could play with us! Anyway, we have something for you, ditch dog."

Willy and Billy began digging into their deep, dirty pockets. They managed to carry an assortment of items that only young boys could call treasures. Billy soon produced a slightly eaten sausage, which he threw toward Ditto; Ditto caught it easily in his mouth. Shortly afterward, Willy threw a half eaten and rather squashed chicken sandwich in Ditto's direction, but his aim wasn't so good. Willy quickly ran forward, picked up the sandwich, and took it directly to Ditto, who eagerly gobbled it up also. Ditto licked his mouth and wagged his tail as Willy patted him on the head.

Janet then said it was time to go as their mother was expecting them home. All the boys came forward and patted Ditto as they said goodbye. Blackie still yapped for attention, and the two younger boys continued their argument. In moments, the noisy crowd was gone. They were always the same. It felt like a hurricane had hit when the Rawlinson kids were around. Ditto had long ago noticed how everyone on the common avoided them when they ran through the village, but Ditto liked their noise and excitement. He thought they were okay. However, he often wondered why he had never seen their mother. The other children usually had a grown-up with them when they walked their dogs.

CHAPTER THREE

Friends on the Common

The next to stroll by was Harold the Boxer dog and his owner, Major Purdy. They were the exact opposite of the Rawlinson kids. Major Purdy was a proper gentleman; tall and distinguished. He always wore a dark green or navy blue tweed jacket with leather patches on the elbows, and a brown leather cap. Ditto liked the way he bowed and raised his cap to the ladies as they passed.

Harold was a well-kept light brown Boxer with perfect manners; he was respectful and had a kind personality. He would never think of pulling on his leash. Instead, he walked tall and proud precisely in step beside Major Purdy. They always said hello to Ditto. Sometimes they had a treat for him, but usually not. Today, however, Major Purdy carried a large, crisp, brown paper bag. As they turned together in perfect harmony and greeted Ditto, they continued to stay precisely in step. Ditto watched as they walked toward him, before together stopping several feet away. Opening the large, crisp, brown paper bag, Major Purdy produced a big, juicy bone. It smelled delicious! Ditto could already taste it, but he remained calm and waited. They would never think of patting Ditto, but Ditto couldn't help wagging his tail even faster, beating it from side to side as he saw and smelled the special treat they'd brought him. Major Purdy raised his hat as he acknowledged Ditto's obvious appreciation, and Harold winked at Ditto. Then they turned, and falling perfectly into step, walked away. They had not gone far when Ditto heard Harold comment to Major Purdy.

"I think the ditch dog will enjoy that, Major Purdy, Sir."

"Yes, Harold. It was an excellent idea of yours, absolutely topper. Nevertheless, I must say that ditch dog could do with a jolly good bath. He smells like a swamp, positively yes he does. By Jove, a swamp, indeed yes. . . Why, underneath his dirty coat I do believe there lurks a rather handsome brown or maybe black and white English Springer Spaniel, indeed I do! What do you say, Harold, old chap?"

As their voices drifted away, Ditto crunched and chewed loudly on the big, juicy bone. He was enjoying his treat so much that he hardly cared what they were saying, but he'd heard enough to think about having a bath. He hated the cold stream water, but if they thought he smelled like a swamp, he would bathe for his friends. Once a year was enough, although Ditto knew it had been much longer than a year since his last bath. Anyway, hadn't he leaped into the stream just this morning when he'd nearly caught a butterfly? At least his legs were clean. He went back to enjoying his bone; crunching and chewing as he kept one eye open, watching for more of his favorite friends.

"Hello, ditch dog." Ditto immediately recognized two very familiar voices. Looking up, he saw little Mandy Bannerman holding tightly onto Wally's leash. Wally was a Pembroke Welsh corgi, and like all corgis, he had bright eyes, perky ears, and a stomach very close to the ground. Once, Ditto had dared ask Wally why his stomach was so close to the ground. Wally was most offended. He'd replied that as a corgi, he was probably related to the royal corgis; and as such, he didn't much care what his stomach was close to!

Wally was a very well behaved little dog, if somewhat stuck-up and boring. Ditto definitely liked the Bannerman family more than he liked Wally. However, he always tried to remember his manners, as he happily greeted them all. Mrs. Bannerman was a kindly woman with a pretty face and gentle manner. She was attractive, tall, and slim; sometimes, like today, she wore a small red hat perched precariously on one side of her head. It constantly looked like it was about to fall, but somehow never did.

Mandy was about six years old. Today, her blond hair was tied tightly in two pigtails on either side of her small face by large, droopy lilac ribbons. The thing Ditto always noticed about Mandy was her dimples. When she smiled broadly, they disappeared; but the moment she stopped smiling they were there again, neatly sitting in her chin. What funny things dimples were! Mandy had the only dimples Ditto had ever seen.

Today, Ditto was delighted to see Sandy had joined them. Sandy was Mandy's nine-year-old big sister. Sandy looked exactly like her mother except she was not as tall. Ditto liked Sandy the most; she never judged Ditto and always gave him a big hug. Today was no exception, and Mrs. Bannerman took Sandy's arm as together they moved toward the ditch. Sandy always wore dark glasses over her eyes and carried a white stick—she was blind. Ditto moved forward out of the ditch so Sandy wouldn't stumble on the uneven surface. Bending down, Sandy felt for Ditto and wrapping both her arms tightly around him, hugged him close. When she released him, she ruffled his coat with her hand. She'd brought him a handful of doggie treats. He eagerly licked them from her hand, his juicy bone momentarily forgotten.

"Well, ditch dog, I came in first in my doggie obedience class today! Mandy, show him my ribbon," Wally said proudly, as Mandy produced the largest blue ribbon Ditto had ever seen.

"We're very proud," added Mrs. Bannerman.

"Oh yes, we are! Wally's such a clever dog! He's smarter, more handsome and cleverer than all the other dogs at doggie training school," said Mandy, giving Wally a huge hug.

"Yes, ditch dog, I also got a new doggie harness. It's so very comfortable," Wally added proudly, moving slightly closer to Ditto so he could get a better look at his shiny new black harness.

"Well, ditch dog, I guess you'll never go to doggie training school. It's only for dogs that are loved—real dogs with real homes and loving families. You're just a dirty old ditch dog who no one wants and no one loves," said Wally none too kindly. Sandy immediately came to Ditto's rescue.

"Wally, that's just not fair! I know Ditto could have a home and a loving family any time he wants to. He could come home with us right now and go with you to doggie training school in the morning, couldn't he, Mummy?" Sandy asked.

"Why yes, Sandy, I guess he could. Another dog in the house would be okay if your father allows it," Mrs. Bannerman concluded.

"Oh Mummy, that would be grand! Then Wally can be my dog and the ditch dog could belong to Sandy. That would be such fun! Oh, do say yes, ditch dog! Do say yes!" Mandy begged, moving closer to Ditto as she held tightly onto Wally's leash.

All dogs are blessed with exceptional hearing, allowing them to hear many things humans cannot. At that very moment, Ditto was aware of Wally's low, threatening growl, so he backed a little further into the safety of the ditch before replying. "It's okay, but thanks very much for your kind offer. I really don't need to go to doggie training school or have a family. I'm a free dog, and I go anywhere I want and do anything I choose. I'm very happy being a ditch dog. You see, I once had a family who I thought loved me, but one day they left town and told me I wasn't going with them. They abandoned me. I now understand how you must first know love before you can have a broken heart, and mine was badly broken. So thank you again, Mrs. Bannerman, Mandy, and Sandy, but I'll stay a ditch dog and see you all whenever you walk on the green." Ditto was looking directly at Wally as he spoke. He knew Wally was a boring dog, but he also knew Wally was a smart dog. As he stared into Wally's eyes, he saw the fear of abandonment looking back at him. It was the same fear

Ditto had felt three long years ago, and it was the same fear Ditto never wanted to feel again.

"That's very sad, ditch dog. I hope you'll change your mind one day. I know Sandy would love you very much," Mandy said, the sadness apparent in her large blue eyes.

"Say goodbye now, girls. We must hurry home or we won't have time for Wally's game of catch." Mrs. Bannerman said as she turned with Sandy to walk away.

"Here, ditch dog, I almost forgot. This is for you," Mandy said, digging deep inside her backpack. She quickly unwrapped a large piece of slightly chewed steak. As she placed it on the ground, Ditto saw Wally hungrily eyeing the tasty morsel. As quick as a flash, Ditto retrieved it into the ditch and out of Wally's reach. After all, thought Ditto, Wally was on the end of a very short leash, and he wouldn't want to disgrace himself by tugging on it as he tried to steal Ditto's treat.

"Thank you all very much," Ditto said, thumping his tail still faster. They all said goodbye as they walked away.

In the distance, Ditto could just make out his most favorite friends. Yes, he was sure: it was Grandma Pippa, Molly, and Miss Pooh, their cute, fluffy white Shih Tzu. Their faces danced before his eyes, as he thought of the way their cheeks glowed when they were warm or very cold, and the way Grandma Pippa and Molly's deep blue eyes crinkled at the corners and sparkled when they laughed. Ditto had always loved them, and his tail wagged furiously as they approached. He loved them so much he was unable to keep his front legs from jumping around with excitement.

CHAPTER FOUR
Last Winter

Last winter, Grandma Pippa, Molly, and Miss Pooh had allowed Ditto to stay in the old garden shed behind their cottage after he'd been rudely thrown out of his hole in the side of the hill. He hated remembering the two foxes who had confronted him, saying it was their home and he wasn't welcome and had better leave. Ditto had hidden from the snow and wind for almost a month in that hole, so he felt he was entitled to some ownership. He told the foxes he had nowhere else to go. However, the foxes wouldn't listen, and they were quite prepared to fight for the hole they said had been their home every winter for their entire lives.

Ditto was freezing cold, hungry, and tired; it was beginning to snow harder, as he reluctantly walked away from his cozy hole. Ditto was not a fighter, and it was two against one, anyway. The only warmth Ditto felt came from his own hot tears of desperation and self-pity, as they ran down his face and dripped off his chin. Ditto was a proud dog, and he didn't want to admit he needed help. He searched for Badley Badger and Stolly Stoat, but they were nowhere to be found. In fact, Ditto couldn't find anyone outside in the freezing weather. Sadly, that was when he reluctantly admitted he couldn't survive without a little help.

Grandma Pippa, Molly, and Miss Pooh were his very best friends in the whole wide world, but the problem was they lived all the way on the other side of the village—and Ditto's feet were already beginning to freeze. It was then things got really bad: Ditto spotted the dogcatcher in the distance, slowly cruising down the lane. Ditto knew he could easily be spotted; he'd allowed his coat to become rather dirty, while the snow around him was white and fluffy. Without hesitation, Ditto raced into the nearest woods and hid, panting wildly he watched the dogcatcher slowly move out of sight. It was then he realized his feet weren't quite as frozen, and he knew that if he ran fast all the way to Grandma Pippa's cottage, maybe he just might make it before he froze again. So, that's what he did. They were overjoyed to see him and begged him to spend the winter with them, sharing the warmth of their cottage. They promised to look after him and love him while he stayed. But Ditto had his pride and wanted only to use the old garden shed as protection from the snow.

Reluctantly, they gave him an old blanket, a bowl of water, and food each day. Each time they did so they held him close and asked him again to become part of their family, but each time Ditto politely declined. So Ditto spent his winter cozily tucked up in his blanket, warm, dry, and safe in the old garden shed at the back of Grandma Pippa's cottage. As the days warmed, he sat with his head out the door and watched the happy family through the long glass French doors. He saw how kind they were to Miss Pooh and just how much they loved her.

Ditto saw Molly and Grandma Pippa's warm, rosy cheeks as they roasted marshmallows over the fire in the evenings and drank hot chocolate before bed. He saw how they played with Miss Pooh endlessly until she fell asleep by the fire, often with Molly beside her. Ditto watched each Sunday as Molly had her long golden hair washed and patiently dried in front of the fire. Miss Pooh also had her bath and sat in front of the fire beside Molly, drying her fluffy white coat while Molly and Grandma Pippa took turns combing and brushing her. On Christmas Day, they begged Ditto to join them inside the cottage. Molly explained how she, too, was an orphan, having no parents of her own. But Ditto didn't spend Christmas inside the cozy cottage. Instead, he watched as they opened their presents in front of the fire, roasted chestnuts, and ate turkey for dinner. He loved the way Molly's and Grandma Pippa's eyes danced and crinkled up at the corners as they laughed. They were so alike and they laughed easily and often. Ditto's dinner that day was delicious and by far the very best meal he had ever tasted.

It proved a long, cold winter. However, the moment the first signs of spring appeared, Ditto graciously thanked them before eagerly returning to his life as a ditch dog. Soon, the robins, butterflies, and all his friends returned, and Ditto once again enjoyed long, lazy, hazy days in the ditches and meadows that he had grown to love. Several times, he almost caught a butterfly as it fluttered low overhead. Yes, very nearly, but not quite . . .

CHAPTER FIVE
Ditto's Best Friends

Ditto cautiously looked out of his hiding place to see where Grandma Pippa, Molly, and Miss Pooh were. They had stopped some distance away and appeared to be having a rather serious discussion. Ditto was so intent on watching his favorite friends he was startled to hear a very familiar voice.

"I just knew you'd be here, ditch dog!" It was Annie. She was the eldest of the twins, Annie and Maggie. With them today was little Tommy; he was only four years old. He slowly followed his big sisters while dragging his old, blue blanket behind him in the dirt. Annie and Maggie were about thirteen years old. Annie had blond hair and blue eyes, while Maggie had straight red hair and brown eyes. Apart from that, they looked exactly alike and they both had lots of freckles.

Little Tommy, on the other hand, was much smaller, with thick, dirty blond hair that stuck straight up in front, sloppy clothes, even more freckles, and two missing teeth on one side of his mouth. He also had large holes in his shoes. Each time Ditto saw him, more of his little fat toes seemed to peek out. The only thing about little Tommy that was clean was his thumb—and the only reason it was clean, was because he constantly sucked on it. Little Tommy was pigeon-toed and more than a little cross-eyed. He always sucked loudly on his thumb and looked at the ground when he walked, although it didn't stop him from often tripping over his dirty blanket. Little Tommy was seldom allowed out with his sisters, so Ditto knew this was a special occasion.

"Oh, ditch dog, Annie and I have been doing a paper route for the last seven months. That's why you haven't seen us," Maggie paused before Annie continued, "So we can afford you now, ditch dog," Annie broke in. "You see, Daddy said we had to be able to pay to have you registered, groomed, and fed before you could come home with us. We want a dog so badly so we worked almost every day for the last seven months . . ." Maggie said as Annie continued midsentence.

". . . We've been delivering papers throughout the village. Now we have plenty of money. So, ditch dog, we will clean you up and take you home with us right now. You will be our dog, our very own." Annie finished as a giant smile transformed her face. Slowly young Tommy took his thumb from his mouth just long enough to speak, "An when theys goes off to school, you's be my dog then."

"Well, ditch dog, are you ready to come home with us and have your very own family that loves you?" Annie asked, walking toward him.

Ditto backed slowly away as he said, "But I don't want a home. I'm happy just the way I am."

"Oh no, you can't be, ditch dog. Why, you have no one to love you or feed you, and you don't have a real family," Annie said sadly before Maggie finished her sentence again. ". . . so you're not even a real dog."

"But you can have some time to think about it. We know you'll say yes, ditch dog, we just know it. We'll come back Friday, and you can come home with us then," Annie continued, the sadness gone as she now sounded very excited and quite sure of herself.

Just then, Grandma Pippa, Molly, and Miss Pooh arrived, and they all exchanged greetings. The twins and Tommy said goodbye to Ditto as Molly jumped right into his ditch. She wrapped her arms around him, and squeezing tightly, she gave him a huge hug.

"Oh, Ditto, we've missed you!" Ditto thought Molly quite adorable. One of his favorite things was the way her pretty deep blue eyes crinkled at the corners and sparkled when she smiled, and she smiled all the time. She had a tiny turned-up nose and the cutest chin Ditto had ever seen.

"Oh yes," Miss Pooh added. "We've missed you a lot and it's actually all my fault."

"No it's not, Miss Pooh. It's our fault, both of us. Anyway, I was the one who threw the ball too hard; it went straight through the hedge and landed in the lane. Grandma Pippa has always warned us."

"Now both of you, why don't you just tell Ditto the reason we didn't visit him yesterday?" Grandma Pippa added kindly before continuing, "It's much too late for blame, and blame never solves anything anyway. Only selfish people blame, and I know, there are no selfish people here now, are there? Anyway, we're all okay."

"Well," began Miss Pooh slowly, "I did what I was not allowed to do. I chased the ball right into the lane. But I caught it, Ditto! I caught it!" Miss Pooh finished proudly in her pretty, refined, girly voice. Like everyone who saw her, Ditto loved Miss Pooh. She was the perfect dog.

"I threw it much too hard and rather too high also," Molly explained. "We were having so much fun. You see it was just at that moment Grandma Pippa went off to answer the phone. We had to stay home yesterday; it was our punishment and the reason we didn't visit you, Ditto. We're both so sorry, Grandma," Molly said, looking very sad as Miss Pooh tried to do the same. Miss Pooh was a fluffy white Shih Tzu, by far the cutest, sweetest, fluffiest dog Ditto had ever seen. He had trouble taking his eyes off her. Today she wore a large, deep pink bow in her hair that matched her pink collar, the sparkly stones dazzling in the sunlight.

"All is forgiven. I know you will both be more careful with the ball in future. Miss Pooh, Molly, let's talk to Ditto about what we discussed earlier," Grandma Pippa said, suddenly sounding much too serious for Ditto's liking.

"Grandma, don't forget what you have for Ditto!" Molly said, winking at Ditto.

"Oh dear me. Why yes, I almost forgot! You're really going to enjoy this, Ditto."

'Oh yes, I know you'll enjoy it, what dog wouldn't?" Miss Pooh added.

"It was really for Miss Pooh, but she insisted we bring it to our friend Ditto. Miss Pooh was worried you might not have enough to eat. Although you look very well feed to me," Grandma Pippa remarked laughing as she produced a half-eaten leg of roast beef wrapped roughly in newspaper from her large, brown handbag. Both Ditto and Miss Pooh started to salivate at the smell and sight of the delicious meat as Grandma Pippa gave it to Ditto.

"Oh thank you! It looks delicious! You always bring me the very best treats," Ditto said, his tail wagging about as fast as it possibly could.

"Well, Ditto, we've been discussing you, and we're worried about you," Grandma Pippa began, tucking a stray gray curl up under her worn brown hat.

"Yes, Ditto. We love you, and we care about you being warm and safe," Miss Pooh added.

"I'm alright. In fact, I'm really very happy. I almost caught a butterfly this morning, just nearly, almost," Ditto boasted, a large smile on his face as he recalled the morning's butterfly chase.

"Well now, Ditto, the thing is, winter's coming again; as you can tell, autumn has already begun. The nights are cooler, and there's a certain nip in the air that hasn't been present for some time," Grandma Pippa continued as Molly added, her eyes sparkling, "'Yes, Ditto, we want you to come and live with us this winter, really live with us in the cottage. We worry about you, and we want you to be part of our family. You can leave at the end of the winter if you still want to and we won't stop you."

Grandma Pippa moved closer to Ditto. "You can't stay out in the cold this year. You're welcome in the garden shed again, of course, but, Ditto, there's plenty of room for another dog and plenty of love to go around."

'Please, Ditto, please!" Molly and Miss Pooh said together as they stared with serious faces at Ditto. Somewhere deep inside Ditto thought just maybe they were right, but he had his pride and his freedom and he valued both very much. If he needed to, he'd move into the garden shed again this winter, and he told them so.

They all looked sad when they heard Ditto's answer but didn't try to convince him further. Finally Grandma Pippa said she'd let him sleep on it and they'd see him tomorrow. Molly hugged him tightly, Grandma Pippa ruffled his floppy ears, and Miss Pooh came very close and kissed his nose, although Ditto had to bend down for her to do so. Then slowly they walked away, turning every so often and waving to him. For the moment, Ditto had quite lost the taste for the treat they had so kindly given him. For a long time, he sat in the deep ditch and thought about what they'd said. The sun was beginning its descent, and Ditto knew it was time to start heading home to his ditch under the old weeping willow tree.

As he was about to leave, he heard Jacky, Macky, and their owner, Lady Barton-Lind, walk past. They never stopped to talk. They were Jack Russell Terriers after all, and therefore, much too upper class to bother talking with an old ditch dog. However, Jacky, Macky and, Lady Barton-Lind nodded in his direction as they passed. Ditto could clearly hear what they were saying.

"Well," said Macky, "I, for one, am very excited about becoming a daddy!"

"I want to be a mummy too,—but Macky, it's a very big responsibility. It's not all fun, you know." Their voices faded away as they continued their walk around the common. Ditto smiled at the thought of Jacky and Macky becoming parents and wondered what Lady Barton-Lind thought of the idea.

CHAPTER SIX
Ditto's Cold Bath

Shortly after Macky and Jacky passed by, Ditto enjoyed the last morsels of his delicious bone. He licked his mouth thoroughly before peeping out of his hiding place. With the leg of roast beef firmly in his mouth, he bounded off in the direction of the stream. He went directly to the deep swimming part. As much as he hated the cold water and the thought of taking a bath, he valued his friends Major Purdy and Harold more; so if they thought he needed a bath, he would do it for them. After leaving his dinner safely on the bank, he closed his eyes tightly and raced toward the stream. He jumped high into the air, and with a loud splash, he landed in the chilly water. Ditto rose easily to the surface and swam around several times before washing his face and behind his ears. The water around him was very dirty, but Ditto didn't believe the dirt could possibly come from his coat. After swimming for a while longer, he noticed the water around him was not quite so dirty. It was, in fact, almost clear.

That was enough for Ditto! He leaped onto the grassy bank and shivering slightly, he shook himself for several minutes before retrieving his dinner. He then found a warm place in the late afternoon sun. He felt the warm sunlight as it penetrated his cold, wet fur. He concentrated on his delicious meal while the sun did its work drying his coat.

His meal was finished long before his coat was dry. Ditto hated the feeling and the smell of wet fur, so he stood up and shook himself some more, trying not to feel the dampness as it seeped into his bones. The sun had dropped lower in the sky as Ditto headed for the long grass and the journey homeward. As he emerged into his favorite meadow, he immediately heard familiar giggles and laughter. Sure enough, it was Stolly Stoat, Badley and Betty Badger, and Ruby Bunny Rabbit with her teenage children. They were all having a great time playing chase in the meadow as the sun prepared for bed.

"Come and join us, Ditto! We thought you'd never come home," called Stolly Stoat.

"Thought the humans might have told the dogcatcher where to find you," Badley Badger added kindly in his deep raspy voice.

"But we're glad you're safe," Betty Badger added.

"You look very clean and handsome," commented Ruby Bunny Rabbit's youngest daughter, shyly winking at Ditto before looking away. Ruby Bunny Rabbit quickly cuffed her youngster over the ear.

As the sun set on the meadow, all the animal friends enjoyed a fast game of chase, although, Ditto noted, there was more giggling than chasing. In no time at all, Ditto's coat was completely dry— although he was too busy racing around the meadow to notice.

It wasn't until much later that Swirly Squirrel reminded them it was already getting dark and way past their bedtimes. Quickly their game ended, and shortly afterward, everyone retired to their own homes for a long night's sleep.

"Good night, Ditto," called Swirly Squirrel.

As Ditto opened one eye to reply to his little friend, he stared in wonder at the millions of twinkling stars above him.

"Swirly!" Ditto called softly into the night. "Swirly, look up at all the stars! Look up into the sky!" There was no answer. Swirly Squirrel was already fast asleep.

Chapter Seven
When Autumn Turns to Winter

It was now early November. The leaves had long since turned from gold to red, as the chilly winds harshly stripped them from the trees. Ditto had long ago turned down Annie and Maggie's offer of a home. He'd also thought long and hard about living with Grandma Pippa, Molly, and Miss Pooh in their cozy cottage, but chose to graciously decline. However, he'd kept the offer of the garden shed open, should he need it later.

Not many people or dogs walked regularly on the common any more, but Major Purdy and Harold still did; unless it was raining or snowing, they'd be walking. The Rawlinson children often turned up also, looking even scruffier as time went by. Blackie seemed more and more out of control, although his tail remained neatly trimmed in a precise round ball. Janet now wore an old red scarf over her holey, pink T-shirt, a moth-eaten red woolen hat, and dirty purple gloves, while Billy and Willy wore heavy parkas and gloves.

Donny and Ronny looked cold and wet in their thin, dirty T-shirts as they held a large umbrella with a hole in one side. Ronny clung shivering to his big brother's trouser leg, while trying to stay dry and warm. Ditto realized they only owned two jackets and seemed to alternate; Ditto saw them on a different child each time. They obviously shared all they had. Ditto understood the Rawlinson family was very poor, but he admired them for taking care of Blackie and one another. They were a happy bunch, if somewhat loud and excitable. They seemed to blow in and out of Ditto's life like the wind.

As November progressed, the days got shorter, colder, and wetter. Ditto could almost smell the coming snow in the air. He went to the village whenever it wasn't raining, but it was harder and harder to hide in his ditch—it was beginning to fill with icy water. Ditto got fewer and fewer treats, but that didn't bother him so much; he was more concerned at not seeing Grandma Pippa, Molly and Miss Pooh since they'd asked him to stay with them. Ditto hated the thought that they were angry with him. He loved them so much! He felt a deep sadness and held a big ache in his heart each evening as he walked back to the old willow tree, which had long since lost its leaves. He knew he would soon need to visit their cottage, and he would try and tell them how sorry he was for rejecting them. Ditto fully realized how precious their friendship was, and the thought of his best friends not being in his life was overbearing, he loved them too much. Nevertheless, he would go to the village for a few more days yet, as the cottage was much farther away.

The next morning, Ditto woke to see snowflakes sprinkling down to earth. The day was clear, with a deep blue sky and very little wind. Ditto thought of summer as he gazed up into the blueness of the sky through the brown branches of the naked willow tree. He thought of the butterflies he used to chase. He thought of his friend Swirly Squirrel who had long ago hibernated for winter. He thought of Stolly Stoat, the Badgers, and all his other friends who were no longer around. But most of all, he thought of Grandma Pippa, Molly, and Miss Pooh and how much he missed them. Again, his heart ached.

Ditto tried to think happy thoughts by telling himself today they might come to the village common to see him, but he no longer really believed it. It had been more than eight weeks since he'd last seen them. He wondered if they'd abandoned him just like the family he'd once lived with, the family who was supposed to love him. However, deep inside he knew they would never do that, not without saying goodbye.

Slowly he uncurled himself from his warm sleeping position, stretched out to become the longest dog he possibly could, went to the stream, and keeping his eyes tightly shut, took a long early morning drink. Oh, but the water tasted cold. He didn't roll in the crisp, frozen grass, as around him more and more snowflakes floated to earth.

Ditto had never spotted the invisible dog again, so he was glad he hadn't made friends with it. Friends should always be reliable—so clearly, the invisible dog was not friendship material. Just to be safe, he never again opened his eyes while he was drinking. The thought was too scary.

CHAPTER EIGHT
Ditto Goes Home

Ditto hid along the end of the common, not far from where he usually sat. Before long, Bruce, the Old English Sheepdog came over to talk. They were going away for the winter, and Bruce was very excited. Despite his heavy coat, both he and Rex loved warmer climates and sunshine. They brought Ditto a bag of treats, a leg of chicken, and a large partly chewed bone. Ditto was very grateful and wished them a safe journey. They waved to him as they walked away.

Ditto always felt a little sad when someone left, but he also felt proud that Bruce was loved enough to really be one of the family and included in their holidays. For a brief moment, Ditto envied Bruce, the family that loved him, and the fun in the sun they were about to enjoy.

No other visitors came to the common for some time. Ditto finished his juicy treats from Rex and Bruce, then snoozed in the winter sun. Most of the snowflakes had stopped, but occasionally a single one landed on Ditto's nose. He hated them landing on his nose most of all. He always tried to lick them off before they melted and trickled down his face.

Ditto was about to fall into a deep sleep when he lazily opened one eye. He thought he saw a small movement way up at the end of the village common; it was the merest of movements that caught his eye. No one else was around, so Ditto raised his sleepy head and looked in the direction of the movement. All of a sudden, he was on his feet, tail wagging eagerly. He narrowed his eyes to make sure what he saw was real.

It was a gray-haired old woman in a brown trench coat; she wore an old brown hat and carried a large handbag and shopping basket. She had stopped to look for something deep in her basket. The trouble was she was at the other end of the common by the village shops. Ditto's tail wagged faster, he was sure now; sure it was Grandma Pippa! He felt a warm happiness bubble up inside. She must be on her way to see him! Sadly, as Ditto watched, she slowly began walking in the other direction. Ditto's heart almost broke; he couldn't believe she was walking away from him and toward the shops.

Without thinking, Ditto shot forward out of the safety of his ditch and raced toward Grandma Pippa. As he approached her, he barked several times to get her attention before she disappeared into the chocolate shop. Please stop, Ditto begged silently; please hear me and stop! He barked again. Sure enough, this time she did stop, and she definitely saw him. She raised her head slightly in his direction and a small smile played on her lips. But it wasn't a large, welcoming smile that crinkled the corners of her eyes like he was used to, just the merest of smiles. However, it was enough for Ditto to know she was pleased to see him, and he bounded up to her. She looked sad, and much older, too.

"Oh Ditto, this is a lovely surprise," she said, ruffling his ear.

"I've missed seeing you. I'm sorry if . . ." Ditto began as he suddenly noticed a single tear rolling down Grandma Pippa's cheek before she quickly wiped it away.

"Why, Grandma Pippa, whatever is wrong?" Ditto quickly asked.

"Ditto, so very much. But it really is good to see you. Molly asks about you every single day."

"But where are Molly and Miss Pooh?" Ditto asked deeply concerned now.

"Molly is in bed—she's been there for weeks. She broke her leg. Tomorrow she finally gets the plaster off, and we hope she'll be able to walk again," Grandma Pippa said, looking even sadder.

"Oh no, why that sounds terrible and very painful. Is Miss Pooh with her?" Ditto asked.

"Oh dear Ditto, I just haven't been able to bring myself to tell you. Miss Pooh and Molly were playing ball in the front garden. Well, it was my fault, I should have been watching. We were all enjoying the garden. I was pruning off the dead flower heads. I wasn't watching for just a few minutes. I didn't see them chase the ball into the lane. The truck driver came around the bend and didn't see them either until it was much too late." Tears freely rolled down Grandma Pippa's rosy cheeks.

"Oh no, you mean . . ." Ditto began, but he couldn't finish. A sob escaped from deep inside.

Suddenly, something tight wrapped itself firmly around Ditto's neck, almost cutting off his breathing!

"Got ya now, you pesky stray! Taken me a while but I's got ya now!" the dogcatcher said. Ditto howled with pain and fright, digging his front legs into the dirt. The dogcatcher dragged Ditto by the neck toward the waiting van.

"Now young man, you stop that at once! That's my dog you have there! Let him go this instant!" Grandma Pippa yelled, racing toward Ditto. The dogcatcher threw him roughly into an empty cage in the back of the van.

Why Mrs., this ain't no one's dog. He's a pesky, dirty, flea-ridden stray and I's been huntin' him for many a long while!"

"Now you listen to me young man! You let him go this instant! He's *my* dog!"

"Now look Mrs., this is very noble of you an' all I'm sure, but he's a filthy animal. Doesn't have no collar, and I bet he's never been registered neither! Anyway, no animals allowed outside without a leash! So where's his leash then, Mrs.?" The dogcatcher sneered, facing Grandma Pippa squarely.

"Young man, I can assure you we just happen to be on our way to the groomers. I admit, he does look a mite dirty, but dogs will be dogs. Now you hand him over to me this instant! Do you hear, me young man? It will be your job on the line! Do you understand me? Your job!" Grandma Pippa's voice was strong and loud.

For several moments, the dogcatcher stared long and hard at her. But she stood her ground and stared right back at him, never blinking or taking her eyes from his. Several more minutes passed, until reluctantly he admitted defeat. Slowly he moved back toward the van. He turned again looking directly at her; he paused for several more seconds, before reluctantly unlocking the cage. Grandma Pippa stood her ground, her hands firmly on her hips, her eyes blazing. The mean, nasty dogcatcher only needed to take one look at her to know she was not a woman to be trifled with.

The very second there was enough room for Ditto to escape, he flew out of the cage, jumping to the ground. He stood as close as he could get to Grandma Pippa, shaking uncontrollably, his tail firmly between his legs. The dogcatcher stood his ground for a few moments longer, as they continued staring each other down. Finally, he retreated to his van and very slowly drove off, all the while eyeballing Ditto in his rear view mirror.

Ditto was shaking, frightened, and thankful all at the same time.

"Oh dear me, what a commotion you caused, Ditto! What are we going to do with you?" Grandma Pippa asked, laughing as she looked down at the frightened dog standing close by her side. It took several moments before Ditto's small weak voice was able to answer, "I really don't know, Grandma Pippa. I belong to you now, so you can decide." Well, the moment those words were uttered, Grandma Pippa finally gave Ditto the big, happy smile he knew and loved, as she bent down and hugged him tightly.

"Oh, Ditto, do you really mean it? You'll make Molly and me very happy! Do you really, truly mean it?" she asked again. Ditto hardly heard her—he was so badly shaken, he wondered if his legs would actually hold him. They felt like rubber. Ditto could only manage to nod his agreement. He was so amazed at just how delighted he had made her.

"So, Ditto, you'll come home with me now?" she asked, and again Ditto nodded. "Okay, then let's see if we can get you into the groomers and clean you up a little, while I get you a proper registration and your very own leash, harness, doggie bowls, coat, and blanket!"

She smiled happily once again. "Oh thank you, Ditto, thank you!" Grandma Pippa said, although somehow Ditto knew he should be the one thanking her.

And so Ditto found himself at the doggie groomers, a place he'd vowed never to go. Somehow, it really wasn't so bad. They used warm water to bathe him and did so several times. Even though Grandma Pippa had instructed them not to trim too much off his coat, Ditto knew they had to cut off quite a lot of his fur because the comb kept breaking. Ditto received a treatment for fleas; he had his nails trimmed and polished, his teeth cleaned, and his tongue scraped. Then he was washed all over again with more nice-smelling liquid and dried with warm air.

After they were finished, he had to admit it was a very handsome dog that looked back at him from the mirror. The fear was almost gone from his eyes, and in its place was the beginning of a happy contented twinkle. Ditto knew he'd had a very close call, and he still couldn't believe he'd escaped. He was one very lucky dog.

The whole grooming procedure had taken nearly two hours. When Ditto was finally ready to leave, they found Grandma Pippa in the waiting room, fast asleep. From the moment she opened her eyes, she was delighted with the result, saying it was certainly worth the wait. She stared in disbelief at the handsome, fluffy, curly-haired white dog with large dark brown patches.

"Oh, Ditto, is that really you?" she asked, hugging him tightly before walking around and around him. Ditto stood proudly, enjoying her admiration.

"Ditto, I do believe you're a pure-bred English Springer Spaniel and a very attractive one at that!" Ditto felt so good, he almost burst with pride. "Well, Ditto, let's put on your new harness and collar with your registration tag and leash. I thought navy blue would look good on you," Grandma Pippa said, sounding almost as excited as Ditto felt. He happily let her place the collar around his neck and the harness over his body.

CHAPTER NINE
Ditto the Real Dog

Before they left the groomers, Grandma Pippa proudly showed him all her purchases. Everything matched, including Ditto's very own coat and blanket; both matched his collar in navy and gray plaid.

"Perfect for a proud dog like you, Ditto," Grandma Pippa said, hugging him once more.

Finally, she paid the groomers, and holding Ditto's leash in one hand and her many packages, handbag, and large basket in the other, left the shop. They stopped just once in the chocolate shop, where Grandma Pippa purchased some of Molly's favorite chocolates for her birthday tomorrow. The girl in the shop came around the counter so she could better admire Ditto, before remarking on what a handsome dog he was. She then asked Grandma Pippa if she may pat him and if he was allowed a small piece of broken chocolate as a treat. Grandma proudly nodded her consent before Ditto eagerly licked the delicious chocolate from the young girls open palm. It was only a small piece of chocolate, but Ditto licked his mouth several times, as he enjoyed the new, sweet taste.

Ditto was surprised at just how comfortable his collar and harness were and happily walked in step with Grandma Pippa, just like he'd so often seen Harold and Major Purdy do. Ditto would never pull on his leash. He was much too proud for that. They walked slowly on for some time, and with each step, Ditto's fear subsided a little more. He knew it was the security of having Grandma Pippa close by his side.

"The groomer really wasn't too bad, Grandma Pippa. It was much nicer than I feared," Ditto commented, walking easily in step beside his new owner.

"Well, Ditto, fear is a strange thing; we all have too much of it. Fear stops us from doing many things in our life. Often fear hides the truth. We all share your fear of change; we'd like everything to stay exactly as it is today and yesterday. I'll bet many of us would like a written guarantee that everything will be just the same tomorrow. Of course, it is a guarantee we can never have. Change is one of the many constant things in life. But you have already conquered more fears than most people know in a life time, and yours were some of the worst."

Ditto said nothing for some time, thinking carefully through what she had just said, before realizing she was right. He had been very scared of change and even more scared of abandonment. But so far the changes were quite easy to handle—much easier than his confrontation with the two angry foxes last winter, anyway. Change was also much easier than his encounter with the dogcatcher. He shivered at the thought. Then he thought about the rest of Grandma Pippa's sentence long and hard before asking, "Grandma Pippa, I don't know what these fears are that you say I've conquered. The ones you say are the worst . . ."

"Oh, Ditto, you were silent for so long I really thought you knew the answer," Grandma Pippa said.

"Oh no, Grandma Pippa, I was just thinking about all you said. Please tell me," Ditto asked, eager to know.

"Ditto, some of the worst fears—for both people and animals— are the fear of abandonment and the fear of not being loved. You've endured both with dignity and pride, Ditto. I, for one, am proud to know you, and I know Molly is also."

Ditto felt a lump in his throat as she spoke; he was feeling very humble and quite unable to answer. After all, Grandma Pippa had just saved his life, waited while he was groomed, and offered him a home, and she had done it all with caring and love. He was so proud of her—but how could he put it into words?

As Ditto walked beside Grandma Pippa, he was beginning to realize just how selfish he'd been. His selfishness had hurt the ones he loved and deprived him of feeling loved also. He'd let the hurt from his past control his future. As a result, he'd almost missed being with the people he loved most.

Molly couldn't believe her ears when Grandma Pippa called up to her that they were home. Molly immediately called back from her bed, asking Grandma Pippa why she'd been so long and why she said *"they."*

"You'll see in about two minutes," Grandma Pippa immediately called back, the laughter evident in her voice.

Quickly they deposited the packages in the kitchen and removed Ditto's harness. Grandma Pippa then found a huge red ribbon and placed it loosely around his neck, before asking him to carry up a small box of Molly's favorite chocolates. Together, they raced up the stairs to where the little girl lay tucked up securely in bed. Apart from her face, the only thing outside the bed covers was her left leg and the huge cast that covered it. Her five tiny toes looked like small pink rosebuds as they protruded from the end.

Suddenly, everything Ditto had been through that day seemed unimportant. He almost cried as he saw Molly's thin tired face light up at the sight of him. She asked several times,

"Ditto, is that really you, is it really you?" She held him so tightly he could hardly breathe, but he didn't care; together Grandma Pippa and Molly cried into his fur. Ditto knew they were tears of joy, and he couldn't help but cry too. Ditto knew he was finally home, exactly where he should be. To Ditto, the ditch dog, at this moment nothing else mattered.

"Oh Grandma, Ditto is the very best present ever! Oh thank you so much, Ditto! Grandma, thank you! Ditto, you really are the very best present in the whole wide world!" Molly cried as, still hugging him tightly, she removed the large red bow and gold chocolate box.

That evening, they had dinner on Molly's bed. It was a joyful, happy occasion. They talked of many things, about the future and all the good times they would share together. To Ditto, the ditch dog, it sounded perfectly grand.

Finally, it was time to say goodnight. Since it was Molly's birthday in the morning and Ditto's first night with them, he was allowed to sleep on the bed with Molly. But from then on his basket and blanket would be on the floor in the corner of her bedroom.

That evening, they all sat on the bed, kissing and hugging each other for what seemed like a very long time.

"Goodnight, Ditto, and thank you so much for loving us and choosing us to be your very own family. You've made this my best birthday ever!" Molly said for the tenth time, her eyes sparkling with happiness.

"It is surely I who should be thanking you. I know now I've made some very silly, childish decisions in my life," Ditto said, feeling very foolish now for rejecting their love for so long.

"Oh Ditto, it's really not about the decisions we make in life but more about what we learn from them that really matters," Grandma Pippa said. "You, Ditto, are very smart. You have endured and learned a lot."

"If I'm so smart, why have I made so many mistakes?" Ditto asked, feeling sorry again for being selfish.

"Actually, Ditto, there are no mistakes in life, only challenges. Remember, Ditto, we all encounter challenges on our journey through life; however, it's only the clever ones amongst us who recognize them, learn our lessons, and move forward. The ability to learn is one of our greatest gifts. Only those among us who tackle life's challenges in a productive and positive way are worth knowing; as we learn we become wiser from our experiences. You have learned many lessons; you are here now, so you have made a wise decision and are a much smarter dog than most. We promise we will never forget that. We love you Ditto," Grandma Pippa said, stroking him tenderly from the top of his head, down his back to the tip of his tail—the same tail that hadn't stopped wagging from the moment he'd entered the tiny cottage.

"We really do love you," added a very sleepy Molly as Ditto realized it must be way past her bedtime.

'Oh yes, Ditto, goodnight. Never fear, we'll always love you," added Grandma Pippa.

"Ditto, I love you very much too," Molly said in a tiny voice sounding almost asleep. Ditto could easily tell she had tears in her eyes.

"It is I, Ditto, the ditch dog, who should say thank you. Thank you for rescuing me and allowing me to be part of your family, loving me, and finally making me a real dog."

"Oh, Ditto," Grandma Pippa began as she brushed the fur from his eyes. "It's not just dogs who need love to be real dogs. It's people also. Only love can make you beautiful, and only love can make you real. Goodnight, Molly, sleep tight. Goodnight, Ditto you sleep tight also, and watch over our precious girl till morning." Grandma Pippa said, turning off the bedside lamp before quietly leaving the room.

Molly had her small arms wrapped tightly around Ditto. He could tell by her breathing she was already asleep.

Ditto, however, lay awake for a long time, thinking. Again he realized just how selfish he'd been and how it wasn't all about him being a free dog, playing chase and catching butterflies. It was about being able to make Molly and Grandma Pippa happy by simply becoming part of their family; caring, sharing, and loving together, each and every day. All this time he'd deprived not only himself of a loving family but those wonderful people who were his very best friends in the whole wide world. Now, together, they made a real family and in turn they made him a real dog. He briefly remembered the long ago family who he'd thought had loved him. But instead of feeling hurt and bitter toward them, he softly thanked them for abandoning him so long ago; because without them, he wouldn't have travelled life's path and ended here, knowing just where he wanted to be.

Before Ditto finally fell into dreamland beside Molly, he was no longer thinking of the butterflies he nearly caught or the game of chase he'd be having with the badgers. Instead, he softly said goodbye and goodnight to all his animal friends, wishing them well. Sadly, he knew this would be the last time he'd ever think of them.

Because, from this moment on, Ditto, the ditch dog, was no more; in his place was Ditto, the loved dog, the real dog. He knew he had so much love to give in return. Ditto now understood it was only love that truly makes you real! Finally, Ditto felt really loved.

As sleep wrapped Ditto tightly in its arms, Grandma Pippa's words echoed again in his mind: *"**It's not just dogs that need love to be real dogs. It's people too. Only love can make you beautiful and only love can make you real.**"*

Goodnight

BOOK TWO
The Hedge Cat

Dedication

To the man whose high expectations and many achievements helped me become who I am today. Your fast life and faster death left your friends and loved ones wanting more. To my brother, John Barr Richardson, whose quick wit, fast temper, and huge ability to love will stay with us always. November 8, 2008, was not only our father's birthday, but also the day you so suddenly left us behind. You taught us how to reach for the moon and hold on tight, through every glorious step of life's journey.

To the many cats who shared your life, this one's for you!

Contents

CHAPTER ONE
Giggles Happy Home

Giggles curled up tightly in her favorite place in front of the fire. It was warm and cozy. She wanted to keep on sleeping, but Paisley, the canary, was singing loudly in his cage just above her head. Giggles had long since given up trying to quiet Paisley and had long since stopped trying to fit her large, fluffy paw between the wire and inside his cage. Paisley was a tease, a horrid, yellow, feathery tease! Giggles knew the very thing that annoyed him most was ignoring him completely, so that's just what she did. Lazily Giggles stretched, very slowly, right out to her full length, claws extended, tail straight. There was no one around to rub her tummy the way she loved, so she yawned widely instead. Finally, she got to her feet and stretched again, as only a cat can stretch.

With sleepy green eyes, she surveyed the room. It was a small, cozy room with too many ornaments cluttering every surface and any tiny space. A collection of various pictures hang from the walls, while too many framed photos were scattered everywhere. It looked almost too full of bric-a-brac, but Giggles loved it all—the old red paint peeling from the walls, as they waited patiently to be covered over by yet another new color; the dusty, worn-out carpet with the many mismatched rugs covering the small holes. Yes, it was a loved room in a loved, cluttered cottage.

It was the only home Giggles had ever known. Giggles loved it all—except, of course, that confounded bird, Paisley! He always managed to know exactly when she wanted to nap. That's when he'd suddenly break forth with the loudest of songs, and his songs went on and on, getting louder and louder. Sometimes they drove Giggles right out her cat door and into the small back garden. But, even curled up tightly with her paws over her ears and in the farthest corner of the garden, she could still hear him. Confounded, bird!

Giggles loved the garden also. It was much like the inside of the cottage, cluttered. Roses, marigolds, herbs, and an assortment of bulbs and bushes crowded the small walled area. Ivy, jasmine, sweet pea, and climbing roses competed eagerly for a place on the crumbling stonewall. While the huge oak tree in the corner seemed to grow taller, every time Giggles tried to climb it. Despite the clutter, the garden was a happy place, and there was always something for Giggles to do or see, or on occasion even chase. Giggles loved the garden best of all when Suzy was home from school and they played together. Sometimes, when she wasn't busy, Mummy came outside and joined them. Occasionally Daddy would arrive home unexpectedly and sit in his old wicker rocking chair, whistling contentedly and watching them play. The garden was a special place, a place where Giggles had the family all to herself. While inside the cottage, Paisley could only watch from the confines of his cage.

Giggles thought Paisley got too much attention anyway. What was so special about him? Sure, he was bright yellow, but he was just a bird after all. Giggles once told him he looked exactly like a painted, yellow sparrow, and sparrows were very common birds indeed. Paisley was most offended, and sat with his back to her for weeks after that. Giggles felt it was one of her greatest triumphs. Anyway, the marigolds were yellow also, and they never got any special attention. Giggles thought it was most unfair, as the marigolds had a much shorter life than Paisley. She felt Paisley lived on and on, singing louder with each passing day.

Giggles stretched again, right out to her full length; she knew it always annoyed Paisley. She then turned on her heels and, with her head and tail held high, she headed for the kitchen without giving Paisley so much as a second glance. Giggles knew Suzy would soon be home from school, but before she took her place on the mat inside the front door, she checked to see if there might be just a drop of milk left in her saucer. She'd checked it several times already, but Giggles was ever the optimist. She knew no one had refilled her saucer, but maybe she'd find a few drops hidden around the edges that she'd missed earlier.

Chapter Two
Giggles Tricks Paisley

At exactly three fifteen each afternoon, Giggles took her place on the mat inside the front door. She sat precisely in the very same place each day, with her large, fluffy white tail wrapped neatly around her freshly bathed, fluffy white body. She sat tall while briefly practicing her purring, she would make sure it was louder and more *purr-fect* than yesterday. It was always the same. The moment Giggles began practicing her purring, that tiresome bird would again broke into song. At exactly nineteen minutes past three, Giggles heard the rusty old hinges on the gate reluctantly move as Suzy pushed it open. Giggles heard Suzy skip the few short steps to the front door; it was the same every day.

The moment the door burst open, Suzy dropped her school bag and books, scooped Giggles up in her arms, before burying her face into the soft white fur on Giggles's tummy and kissing her all over, before telling her just how much she'd missed her. By this time, Giggles was purring loudly and telling Suzy she'd missed her more! Suzy would then throw Giggles high on her shoulder. Giggles held tightly to Suzy's clothes with her front paws, as Suzy's hand rested under Giggles tail. Suzy then scooped up her bag and schoolbooks in her other arm and kicked the door closed with her foot. Still tightly holding Giggles, they walked the few steps to Paisley's cage, and Suzy talked briefly to him before checking his water and seed dish; it was the same each day. Giggles always made certain she was facing the other direction; looking at that tiresome yellow bird while tightly in Suzy's grasp was unthinkable, and quite undignified for a cat of class. However, Giggles knew how Paisley's chest puffed out even further with the attention. Naturally, he broke forth into his very loudest song of the day.

A few moments later, Paisley's time for the day was over. Together Suzy and Giggles headed into Suzy's bedroom. She dumped her schoolbooks on the old bed before, together they collapsed also. The bedsprings squeaked and groaned from the intrusion and extra weight, but no one noticed; it was the same every school day. And that's where Suzy and Giggles stayed as Suzy told Giggles about her day at school: Miss Prim, her funny, short, chubby teacher, whom she loved; the lessons she'd learned; the girls she played with on the playground; and the horrid boys who'd annoyed her. Today Suzy told Giggles how one of the boys had tugged her long braids much too hard and called her "Freckle Face." Suzy said this was the boy she hated most in the whole school. He already had one of his front teeth missing, and Suzy wanted desperately to remove the other, only it just wasn't lady-like, and her friends were watching. Shortly afterward, Suzy changed into still older clothes. At exactly ten minutes passed five, Giggles, still purring contentedly in Suzy's arms, would be happily sitting on the front step, watching and waiting for Mummy's arrival home.

Mummy always stroked Giggles first before kissing Suzy. She then quickly changed from her smart brown or beige suit into her old clothes. Upon entering the kitchen, Mummy took her faded red apron from the hook behind the door and placed it over her head, before tying it in a neat bow behind her back. Suzy and Giggles sat at the table as Mummy busied herself in the kitchen preparing dinner. As Mummy cooked, they all talked about their day, but Giggles never mentioned just how tiresome she found Paisley's company. She knew they loved the yellow bird too. Giggles rubbed lovingly against Mummy's legs just a couple of times. She'd been told previously that too much rubbing and purring distracted Mummy from her cooking. This was the time of the day her dishes were refilled with water, milk, and her dinner. Although, her tummy was growling at the delicious smells, she never touched her food until the family sat down at the dinner table to enjoy their own meal. At exactly six o'clock, Daddy arrived home from work, and soon afterward they dined.

"Now Suzy, I want you to wear your Sunday best to school tomorrow. Take your hat and gloves also, and be very careful not to get them dirty."

"But Mummy, why?" Suzy asked as Giggles stopped eating to lick her lips and listen.

It was Daddy who answered.

"Tomorrow is Grandma's sixtieth birthday, so it's a very special day. Your mother and I are both leaving work early. We'll be waiting for you outside the school gates in the car." Daddy explained as Mummy continued, "Yes, we'll drive straight to Grandma's and arrive in time for dinner," Mummy continued. "I'm making her birthday cake tonight."

"But who's going to give Giggles her dinner, Mummy?" Suzy asked, sneaking a sideways glance at her beloved pussycat.

"Oh, Suzy, we'd never forget Giggles," Mummy said. "She's a very important part of the family. Now, Giggles," Mummy began, turning toward her. "We'll leave extra food in your bowl tomorrow, and you're not to eat it until dinnertime, just like you always do," Mummy said, addressing Giggles directly. Giggles had her mouth full of food and could only nod her understanding.

That evening, as Mummy stayed up late and made Grandma's birthday cake, Suzy and Giggles made her a card. Giggles told Suzy what to write and draw. The card read:

"Happy Birthday Grandma B,

From Suzy
and
White Fluffy Me!"

Suzy then drew a little girl with freckles, bright blue eyes, and long red curly hair tied up in ribbons. She added a large birthday cake and a fluffy white cat. It was a funny-looking card, as the cake was much larger than the two of them. Together they raced into the kitchen to show Mummy and Daddy; together they laughed.

A short time later, the tiny cottage was silent and dark as everyone drifted happily into dreamland. Giggles was supposed to sleep in her basket in the corner of Suzy's bedroom, but Suzy couldn't fall asleep without cuddling her beloved pussycat tightly in her arms. So each night after Mummy finished their bedtime story and turned off the light, Giggles silently jumped onto the bed and curled up inside Suzy's arms. Suzy would instantly fall asleep, while holding her favorite pussycat close.

That night, Giggles purred for a long time as Suzy slept, but Giggles just wasn't sleepy. She thought of all the time she'd spend alone tomorrow with that confounded bird and its noisy singing. The way cats usually pass the time when they are bored is to sleep, but that would be impossible with Paisley around, Giggles thought. As Giggles lay thinking, she suddenly formed an idea. Careful not to wake Suzy, she crept into the living room and silently jumped onto the high back of the old arm-chair. Very slowly, without a sound, Giggles lifted Paisley's night cover just a little at one corner. Silently, she put her head under the canary's cover, moving as close to the cage as she could. She was just inches from the little yellow bird; he slept tightly fluffed up, with his head tucked neatly inside his wing. He was now so close, the smell of warm feathers was almost more than Giggles could bear. When she was as close as she could get to the sleeping bird and in the silence of the house, she let out one very loud *meow!* At the same time, she dropped the cover quickly back into place and leaped from the back of the chair.

Paisley reacted immediately. The cage rocked back and forth as he madly flew around, fluttering his wings wildly against the side while tweeting loudly at nothing. Moments later, Giggles heard movement coming from Mummy and Daddy's bedroom. Quickly she raced back into Suzy's room. She curled up tightly in her basket; she was unable to control her loud purring, but managed somehow to suppress her laughter.

Giggles listened as Daddy put the light on in the living room and lifted Paisley's night cover, chastising the silly bird for making so much noise and disturbing their sleep. Daddy sternly told Paisley that should it happen again, he would have to sleep in the laundry room. Giggles couldn't stop laughing! In fact, she was out of her basket and under Suzy's bed, positively rolling around the floor, laughing. Giggles wondered why she hadn't thought of doing this before? It was definitely the most brilliant idea she had ever had. The best part was that Paisley had absolutely no idea!

CHAPTER THREE
Butterflies

The next morning, there was more activity than usual around the cottage. Everyone took extra care getting dressed so they would look their best for Grandma's birthday. Daddy carefully placed their coats and the large basket containing the cake in the car. Giggles got extra cuddles from everyone before they left. She was instructed not to wait up, as they'd be home very late. Mummy reminded Giggles again not to eat all her food until dinnertime or she'd be hungry all evening.

Giggles didn't want them to go, so she asked if she could come with them. She reminded them that she was very good at sleeping, waiting, and generally sitting still. She'd been in the car several times before, and even though she really didn't like the motion, she was quite happy when the car was still; it had all the smells of home. It was really quite comfortable.

Suzy thought this a perfectly super idea—this way, she wouldn't need to worry about Giggles as she'd be right there with them. However, Mummy and Daddy said it was a very long journey and maybe Giggles could come with them on a shorter trip one day soon. Giggles sat with her nose pressed tightly against the window and watched as they drove away. She stayed at the window until they were long out of sight; she missed them already. Now it was just her and that pesky, singing, yellow bird . . . oh, could the day get any worse? Giggles sulked as she sat looking out the window at nothing at all.

As the time went by, the day did get worse—and still worse. The embers of the fire died down completely until it was hardly warm at all, and every time Giggles dozed off, Paisley broke forth into song. His songs seemed to go on forever. Giggles only managed a short nap on Suzy's bed, even though she knew she wasn't allowed in there during the day. She worried that Paisley, the horrid bird, would tell on her.

It was about three o'clock in the afternoon, the time Giggles usually prepared for Suzy's arrival home from school, but today there was nothing to look forward to, and she was beginning to feel very bored. She strolled into the kitchen and finished the last of her food. She then decided she deserved to drink all her milk—after all, she didn't have anyone's arrival to look forward to, not until much later anyway. Paisley had been even more annoying than usual, claiming he was composing yet another new song. Giggles was becoming increasingly irritated with the bird and his songs, but most of all with his arrogant, conceited, yellow self. Giggles needed to get away for a while; the family wouldn't be home for many hours. She wandered outside into the garden. The sun was warm and the flowers happy. She sniffed the air; there had to be more going on out here than inside the cottage.

Giggles wandered over to the large oak tree; she liked to lay in the sun in a hollow between the roots. The flowers were all friendly, and as she passed, they nodded their brightly colored heads in a happy hello. Giggles stretched out in the sunshine. It felt warm on her fur; birds chirped quietly high up in the tree, and life was good.

Giggles fell into a light sleep until, suddenly, something landed on her nose; it tickled. She jumped to her feet as her front paw wiped her nose and she opened her eyes. It was then she saw a beautiful, bright blue butterfly hovering nearby, obviously wanting to play. She tried to swipe it with her paw, but each time it fluttered just out of her reach.

It landed on the marigolds, and Giggles raced over to catch it; then it fluttered onto the tall stems of the ginger flowers, and she leaped high into the air, only just missing it. Round and round the garden they went; each time she almost caught it. What a prize, Giggles thought, if she could take the butterfly inside and show Paisley. The beautiful butterfly fluttered onto the warm stone wall, and Giggles jumped high and nearly caught it again. From there it flew up into the oak tree and sat at the end of the branch that grew over the garden wall and into the meadow beyond. It just sat there calmly, opening and closing its wings in the sunshine. Giggles had never quite managed to jump high enough to get onto the bottom branch, but today she was so intent on catching the butterfly, she easily made it. She quickly ran the full length of the long low branch. When she was nearly at the end, it tipped slightly toward the ground.

Again, the butterfly fluttered away, and without realizing what she was doing, Giggles was chasing it across the meadows in the long, lush, green grass. So intent was Giggles on catching the butterfly, she hadn't noticed where she was. Giggles had never been over the wall before. On and on she ran. Every so often, she leaped high into the air, almost touching the pretty, blue butterfly. She loved the game! Then, to her delight, there were *two* beautiful blue butterflies, fluttering side by side. They flew together high into the air before fluttering close to the ground, occasionally stopping on a blade of grass or a tree branch, while opening and closing their wings in the warm sunlight. Giggles loved running fast. She loved the feel of the wind as it blew her whiskers against her face and pinned her ears back against her head. Giggles ran faster and faster. It was exactly what she had to do just to keep up!

CHAPTER FOUR
How Lost Is Lost?

A long time later, the two beautiful butterflies flew high into the sky, higher than they'd ever flown before. Giggles suddenly realized she was tired. She stopped where she was and stared. Right in front of her, looming tall and dark, were the tallest, thickest trees she'd ever seen. At their bases grew tangled shrubs and dark undergrowth. Giggles immediately saw how the grassy meadow ended and turned into the dark, forbidding woodlands; she shivered. Looking up, she noticed the sun was low over the trees and she could easily feel a crisp nip in the air. Giggles was a young pussycat who'd never before even ventured out of her front gate by herself—let alone over the back wall. She knew today's adventure was definitely over.

Strange, new, and different noises came from deep within the woodlands; shadows and scurrying creatures Giggles could hear but couldn't see. The occasional flicker of fading sunlight through the tall trees and the rustling of unknown sounds in the undergrowth were enough to alert a loved house cat to danger! Giggles felt very afraid. She didn't want to go anywhere near the woods; all she wanted to do was go home, to her empty dinner plate, cozy basket, and comfortable cottage. Maybe even home to Paisley. But thinking about him a little more, she decided he wasn't one of the things she was missing after all.

As she stood at the edge of the woods, a low howling startled her. She retreated a few steps backward into the sunshine of the meadow. Her eyes darted everywhere; big, scared, green eyes, wide with fear. Her ears flicked this way and that, trying to catch all the new sounds and decide where they were coming from. The fur on her back spiked, as her tail involuntarily twitched.

Giggles knew it was time to head home, and fast! She turned around and around, but all she could see was the grassy meadow, the occasional tree, and a few patches of yellow and blue flowers. The only thing she was sure of was that through the woods was not the way home. That left her three options. But, as she looked in each direction she saw more grass, miles and miles of tall, lush, green grass bending slightly as the breeze rippled through it.

Giggles had no idea which way was home; nothing looked familiar. She tried to see the trail she had left behind her, but quickly realized the lazy breeze had taken it away. Again, another sound from deep within the woods scared her, and this time she started running, nowhere in particular, but away from the noises within the woods. Giggles couldn't believe the two pretty butterflies had gone into the woods, but then she remembered just how high they'd flown and she understood they must have flown above the tall trees. Giggles wondered if she ran fast enough, she, too, might be able to fly. But as fast as she ran, even when the wind pushed her ears and whiskers tight against her head, her feet never left the ground.

Giggles felt tired and hungry. She'd never run so fast, and she'd certainly never run so far. Which way was home? There were no cottages or people anywhere—just lots and lots of grass. Finally, Giggles spied a tall oak tree standing all alone. It had some low branches, and she knew these would make it easy to climb. Without a moment's thought, Giggles raced toward it and jumped as high as she could. She was relieved to find she'd made it to the first branch. From there it was easy; the branches were not too far apart. She was sure she'd be able to spy her cottage from high up in the tall old oak tree.

"Get away from our branch! You leave my family alone!" shrieked a large mother robin, puffing her red breast out and flying at Giggles with her sharp pointed beck. Giggles was shocked and immediately jumped to another branch, away from the robin's attack.

"This is our branch, and you're not welcome here. Go away!" This time it was a pair of blackbirds screeching at Giggles. One swooped low over her fluffy tail and pecked it hard. Giggles yowled with pain and retreated several steps; their beady black eyes followed her.

Giggles wanted to speak, but it took several tries before she found her voice. "I'm not after your family." She sounded frightened and her voice shook as she spoke. "I'm lost and just want to get to the top of the tree and look for my cottage."

"Why, hedge cat, there's no cottages around here unless it's your hedge you've lost," Father Blackbird said none too kindly.

"I'm not a hedge cat; I'm a house cat. I have a home and I am loved," Giggles responded, sounding more confident than she felt.

"Oh sure you are! You don't look loved to me. Why your socks are all green, and so is your underbelly. Your tail is full of twigs and leaves. You're no house cat! You're after our babies!" The angry birds screeched again as they both attacked Giggles. She hurriedly backed away.

Giggles knew it was pointless trying to talk to them, so she jumped higher and further away from their sharp beaks and precious babies. She climbed very high, until looking down toward the ground, she realized how silly she'd been. How was she going to climb down? The sun was almost setting as Giggles searched the horizon for home. All she saw was grass, miles and miles of grass, and behind her the very scary woods.

Chapter Five
The Owls and Pussycat

It was sometime later, as Giggles found herself still higher up the tree on a smooth, wide branch with no one attacking her, that she stopped to survey her situation. The branch was broad, flat, comfortable, and very far from the ground. Each time Giggles looked down, she felt strange inside, so she stopped looking down altogether. Dusk wrapped around her as the night hurriedly chased away the last glimmers of the day. For the hundredth time, Giggles wished she were safely home in front of the fireplace, even if the fire had long since gone out. She wished she were eagerly awaiting the sound of the car pulling into the driveway, the engine stopping, Suzy's soft footsteps, and Mummy and Daddy's too. Sadly, she could only imagine, as Giggles was, for the first time in her life, lost, hungry, cold, and frightened. She didn't know where she was, how to get home, or even how to get down the tree. One lonely, warm tear escaped from the corner of one of her large green eyes. She felt a deep sadness inside until she realized she must try and think just what was good about her situation.

However, the only good thing about right now was that the branch she was on was wide and flat. Giggles did exactly what all cats do when they're thinking or bored; she curled up in a tight, fuzzy, white ball and thought deeply.

"Whoooooo, whooooo do you think it is on our branch? Whoooo, whoooo can it be?"

"Why, it really doesn't matter anyway, Alfie. The white fluffy thing is nowhere near our end of the branch. We have plenty of room. Whooo, whoooo!" came the reply.

"But Ollie, do you suspect it's alive?"

"I don't know and don't care." Ollie replied "It's just a thing but its coat is much whiter than ours. I thought we had the whitest feathers around," replied Alfie Owl, his eyes wide. His round head flicked this way and that before moving in all directions.

"Well, maybe we haven't the whitest feathers after all. Most of our feathers are pale; some are light brown with a few gray flecks. I think we are mainly white anyway, as barn owls should be, and it really doesn't matter that much. We'll just leave the thing alone, and maybe it won't notice us. If we don't bother the thing, the thing probably won't bother us. Whoooo, whoooo," said Ollie Owl, taking a few steps closer to get a better look.

"Come on, Ollie. Come back down our end of the branch. Let's do what we owls do best—watch, listen, and wait," said Alfie, turning his head almost all the way around and then back again.

"I think we should prod it or something, just to see what it is. Whoooo, whoooo."

"Leave it alone, and it will leave us alone."

"But maybe we can eat it or something! Whooooo, whoooooooo."

"Don't be silly. It has way too much fluff, feathers, or whatever. Whoooooo. We'll just watch and wait."

Ollie and Alfie Owl had only just taken their places at the farthest end of the branch when Giggles awoke from a short but deep nap. She'd tried to think but had ended up falling heavily asleep. She slowly stretched a long, lazy stretch, almost losing her balance, as one of her back feet slid off the edge of the branch. Suddenly, a frightened expression came over her face as she remembered just where she was. She'd been hoping it was only a dream, but she felt too cold and hungry for it to be a dream. Looking around, it was also much too dark. Through the smaller branches above her, she saw stars twinkling brightly in the clear night sky. Had she been safe at home, it might have been a pretty sight, but up here in this tall tree, it was frightening to a young house pussycat like Giggles.

Gingerly, she curled her tail around her paws and sat back down on the branch, backing as close as she could toward the trunk. The slight night breeze chilled her nose. It was very dark, and Giggles was aware of the many new and strange night noises all around her. Her fluffy, white ears flicked this way and that as she tried to locate each sound, but before she could do so, yet another grabbed her attention. Her green eyes were wide in the darkness, and even though cats are supposed to have superb night vision, Giggles had spent most of her nights curled up asleep safely on the end of Suzy's bed. As she sat and watched, her eyes gradually became accustomed to the inky darkness.

Very slowly, she moved her face this way and that, until suddenly she got the fright of her life, as two round pairs of dark brown eyes stared directly at her. They were only about six feet away, and they looked enormous! The two pairs of eyes appeared situated in round white faces that looked like large, white, china saucers. Instead of a nose and mouth, they had thin pinkish beaks. Giggles felt so frightened she almost fell off the branch. Her back feet jumped backwards, so she now needed to climb back down securely onto her branch again. She shook uncontrollably. She was unable to stop shaking; she pressed herself hard up against the trunk. Her eyes were almost as wide as thiers. She stared, her tail twitching. She waited. She was unable to move even if she'd wanted to. The first noise the creatures with the huge eyes made scared her beyond words.

"Whooooooooo, whoooooooooooo," the eerie noise was loud and strange. Frightened, Giggles did nothing; she waited and watched. Gradually, she made out the rest of the shape attached to the noise.

It seemed to be large and wore a neatly mottled coat of light brown with speckles of gray. She thought the hood very elegant as it framed precisely around the white feathery face. What very unusual creatures, Giggles thought as she stared. She couldn't see any feet or wings, but since it was up here in the tree she thought it surely must be some kind of rather large bird. Did birds have eyes in the front of their heads? Giggles asked herself. Thinking briefly of Paisley, she decided not. Just then, they made yet another strange eerie noise.

"'Whooooo, whooo are you? Whoooooooo," a voice asked. It didn't seem angry, nor did it sound scared, but what Giggles noticed most was that it didn't seem threatening either. Giggles didn't know what to do. She couldn't move any farther up the tree trunk; her back feet were already horizontal.

"Whoooooooooo are you, and why are you so far up our tree?" asked Ollie kindly. She could clearly tell the thing, was even more scared than they were. Slowly, Giggles managed to find her small voice from somewhere deep inside.

"I'm lost. My name is Giggles. I'm a house cat and I'm lost. I just want to go home!" Giggles voice was tiny as she burst into tears. She'd been trying hard not to, but she was so frightened she couldn't help it. With her face downcast, Giggles sobbed softly, large round tears rolled down her fluffy fur, dripping from the tip of her nose onto her paws.

"But surely with those green socks and underbelly and all those twigs and leaves in your fur, you're a hedge cat who just happened to climb too high. Yes, that's what you are. You'll just have to sleep here until morning. It's too dangerous now to go back to your hedge. Whoooooooooooooo," said Alfie kindly as they both stared at the small, frightened sobbing creature.

"Whoooooooooo! I thought it might be a cat, Alfie. It's really fluffy."

"Yes, my dear, of course you're right. Whoooooooooooo, or rather what, are we going to do with it? It seems harmless enough, and, as you say, rather white," Alfie finished. The owls stood very still and stared as only owls can. Every so often, they turned their heads almost all the way around, before again becoming still.

"I just want to go home! I want Suzy and my milk dish and my place in front of the fire. I'm lost and I don't know how to get home," Giggles sobbed. The owls looked on, feeling sad for the small white cat, but they had no idea what to do.

After a while Alfie asked, "But if you really are a loved house cat, just how did you get out of the house and all the way here? There are no cottages for miles. You really are very lost. Whooooooooooo!"

"House cats don't just live inside a house. I have my very own cat door, you know." Giggles paused as a loud sob escaped her before she continued, "Anyway, it was the butterflies! I thought I loved them, but now I hate them!" Giggles said as her sobs slowed but didn't quite stop.

"But surely, if you really are a loved house cat, you wouldn't want to run away. It sounds to me like you had lots of friends and people who loved and cared about you. Why, it is a very special thing to be loved and cared about. In fact, those are the most precious things in the whole world. Love and friendship make you real inside. We know, as we owls are the wisest things in the whole world, aren't we, Alfie?"

'Yes, my dear, we certainly are. We have respect for every living thing, and we never judge without fully clearing our minds and listening carefully. Why, we'd even listen to the butterflies' side of the story, although butterflies are awake in the daytime when we're usually fast asleep, so we've never actually seen one. Whooooooooooooo," Alfie finished.

These strange birds seemed to be the kindest things Giggles had found so far, so she relaxed a little—just a little.

"You're the nicest things I've met since I've been lost," Giggles said. "Would you be my friends?" Giggles hastily asked, hoping desperately they'd say yes. She felt like everything was against her right now, and Giggles knew she really needed someone on her side.

"Well now, little hedge cat—Giggles—you see, friendship is not really something you can ask for. Friends can't be purchased; you're not automatically born with any, and no one can be your friend unless they truly want to. You see friendships must be earned," said Alfie.

As Ollie continued, "Yes, little hedge cat, Alfie's right; he's a very wise owl indeed. Whooooo, whoooooooooooo. You seem nice enough, but you say you are a cat, and everyone around here knows Emu, the devious old hedge cat. No one likes him, and he doesn't have any friends. You see, he's not a very trustworthy hedge cat". Ollie added as Alfie continued, "Yes, but I know you're not like him; I can just tell. Nevertheless, in your travels you must be very wary of Emu, the hedge cat. He is not to be trusted. We shall think about being your friend, little white hedge cat," Alfie said.

"In the meantime, we very much respect you and think you're quite nice," Ollie said. "We know you're not like Emu at all, but trust is another one of those things you must earn. We wonder if you know the meaning of loyalty also. Trust and loyalty go together like night and day. They are both different but complement each other at the same time. We are very wise old owls, Giggles, whoooo, whooooooo are trying to help you. Alfie will fly around the village and see if anyone has been asking about you. Maybe there's a better hedge closer to the village; if there is, he will be the one to find it. But for now, we'll show you a hedge where you can hide. It's not far from here. You are, after all, a white cat, and easily spotted against the green grass from a long distance. Whoooo, whoooooo." Ollie said.

They talked for some time. The owls explained who they were and promised again to help Giggles find her way home. They told Giggles she must survive by eating snails and slugs. In the morning, she must quickly find a safe place under a wide, deep hedge in case the foxes should hunt her. They pointed the way she must run when morning arrived, and they said again they'd fly over the village to see if anyone was looking for her. Giggles described Suzy in detail before sobbing again, as she realized how much she missed her. Finally, the owls said they had to stop talking as their great wisdom came mainly from watching, listening, and thinking, and not so much from talking.

Night was moving on, and they were getting hungry. Giggles slept for a while, feeling safe under their gaze. It seemed like little time had passed before Alfie woke her with an early morning gift of several fresh snails. He laid them neatly in a line on the wide branch in front of her and told her she must eat them. Giggles had only ever seen snails slowly crawling around the garden. They weren't much fun at all. In fact, when she tapped their shells with her paw, wanting them to move faster, they stopped altogether and retreated quickly into their shells. She'd never thought of eating them. However, she was starving, so closing her eyes tightly she crunched hungrily on the snails, shells and all, before swallowing quickly. The owls then presented her with two very large fat slugs, which she also quickly devoured.

As morning brightly broke, the birds' chorus announced the beginning of a new day, and the owls said it would soon be their bedtime. They again showed Giggles the direction of the hedge grove, saying that even if she couldn't see the hedge from here it was over the small hill, and she must run fast all the way. Alfie promised he would find her if he located her cottage. Giggles thanked them as she quickly washed her front paws. She usually had a leisurely bath each morning and evening, but at present, it was the furthest thing from her mind. She had tried to avoid looking down until finally she gained enough courage to look cautiously toward the ground. Giggles discovered it was, indeed, a very long way down!

CHAPTER SIX
Giggles, the Hedge Cat

The sun was high in the sky by the time Giggles navigated her way down the tree. If she didn't look at the ground, she wouldn't feel that strange scary feeling in her stomach. So, she carefully took it branch by branch. She missed her footing just once but didn't fall far; it was her prowess as a cat that was damaged more than her fluffy body. How much easier this would be if she were home! There, if she climbed too high, all she needed to do was meow loudly and Suzy or Daddy would come and rescue her.

Once safely on the ground, she felt the sun's warmth penetrating her fur. Her shaking had almost subsided. She raced through the slightly moist, green grass, hoping desperately that she was heading in the right direction. The grass was so much taller than it appeared from the tree. She could hardly see just where she was heading. Everything looked different down here. A large orange butterfly floated by, just above her head. Giggles leaped high into the air but missed it, then bounded after it. She hadn't gone far, however, before she remembered her plight, so she stopped exactly where she was and tried to remember the direction from which she had just run.

After carefully thinking for several minutes, she felt sure she knew the way to the hedge. The long grass tickled her nose, the smell fresh and crisp as it ascended her nostrils. Giggles was running just as fast as she could go. To Giggles, the little house cat, it felt as though she was almost flying. Usually she loved the feeling, but out here in the open meadow, it was fear that drove her, not enjoyment! It seemed like forever before she raced down a small hill, suddenly spying the tall hedge the owls had told her about. Until that moment, Giggles thought she was heading in the wrong direction. She silently chastised herself for chasing the orange butterfly. It was always butterflies that got her into trouble. She would try and hate them, but they were so pretty and the way they teased her as they fluttered through the air!

Suddenly, there it was, directly ahead, a wide, tall, brown, green, and yellow hedge. She couldn't see what the hedge surrounded, but she slowed her pace as she looked for a way inside its tightly woven branches. It was dark and dry, and the twigs scraped against her nose, but she kept going. Smaller animals had already made many passageways. As Giggles pushed her way through, the small branches moved to accommodate her size.

Giggles jumped with fright as loud barking and sniffing shattered the silence. The feel of the hedge moving frantically frightened Giggles even more; she turned in the confined space to face the direction of the noise. She moved backward as far as she could. Through the leaves and branches, she clearly saw a large black snout. Its nostrils flared as they opened and closed; it sniffed loudly in her direction. More barking erupted, closer and louder than before. Giggles could see the front legs of a huge black dog bounding back and forth, back and forth, as it barked and sniffed just inches from where she sat, shaking. Giggles had only seen dogs through the window along with the two she had watched when she'd been out driving in the car with Mummy, Daddy, and Suzy. That was as close as she ever wished to get!

Giggles now knew a dog at such close proximity was horrifying! Big, dirty, and smelly, this dog never stopped moving, and the constant loud, deep barking . . .

"Come on, Sam," a voice said, "there's be no bunnies in that there hedge, not at this time of day. We best be gettin home to the cows. It be about milkin' time soon. Come Sam, come boy!"

Giggles watched silently from her hiding place. He was a tall, skinny man, with wispy white hair poking out from under a dirty, floppy, hat. He bent low over a long stick, as he walked slowly behind the large, bounding, black dog and away from the hedge where Giggles hid.

What terrifying things dogs were! She'd never imagined just how many horrors lay in wait for a small house cat in the outside world. She looked deeper into the gloom of her hiding place. She moved slowly, as space was at a premium. Up ahead, Giggles could just make out a large dead tree trunk that had once grown up through the center of the hedge. This will be safer, she thought. There was slightly more room around the base, so Giggles could easily curl up and sleep.

"Get away from our burrow! Get away, you horrid, green hedge cat!" came the angry words of a large, round, fluffy bunny. It was mainly brown with white patches and had very long, floppy ears. Standing directly behind the biggest bunny Giggles had ever seen was another smaller bunny who added nastily,

"This is our home; we were here first! Find your own! That's what we told Emu, the hedge cat, and that's just what we're telling you. Go away!" said the smaller bunny angrily, while still partly hidden behind the larger one. They both shook their heads at her several times before disappearing into their hole, leaving her staring after them.

It was then Giggles noticed two large, plump slugs slowly climbing up the old tree trunk. She hated the taste, but she was hungry enough to grab them with her paw and quickly eat them. She moved around to the other side of the tree trunk and deeper into the security of the hedge. No one bothered her. It appeared to be safe and dry so Giggles curled up in a tight, furry ball and slept soundly.

It was the sniffing and the movement, along with the unfamiliar, high-pitched yapping that woke her. Giggles had been enjoying the most wonderful dream, in which she was safely home and chasing butterflies around her own garden.

The long, light red snout pushed its way closer to Giggles through the twigs. She could see the dark glint of black, beady eyes; the sniffing was getting closer. Frightened beyond words, she moved away, only to realize that on the other side of the hedge was more sniffing. It was closer now, and she could even feel the warmth of its breath. From where she hid, she saw the thing looked sort of like a small dog, but it yapped and seemed much too aggressive. Then Giggles remembered the owls' warning about foxes. Yes, thought Giggles, these are red foxes. In moments, two became four, all pushing their way toward her. Giggles curled up into a small hole in the ground, staying absolutely still, watching, waiting, and shaking more fiercely than ever. Giggles' eyes were huge in her head, as her ears feverishly flicked around. Sniffing and yapping loudly, the foxes drew nearer.

Giggles was unable to focus on anything but the immediate danger, so she hardly heard the noise of the car engine and car door opening. The sniffing held her focus and was her main fear.

"Giggles, Giggles, are you there? Oh please, Giggles, where are you?" It was Suzy's voice! Suddenly Giggles was sure she was about to be rescued! She sat very still, waiting, and the sniffing abruptly stopped.

"Come on, Suzy girl. She couldn't have come this far. It's almost tea time. Let's go home." It was Daddy's deep voice. She then heard the car door quickly closing, the engine revving, and the car disappearing. Giggles couldn't believe her ears. Not only was she almost rescued and the foxes scared away—but they'd left without her!

Maybe she should have meowed, but no, the foxes were much closer than Suzy. Maybe she should have run out from the hedge, but no, the foxes were waiting to eat her. Giggles curled up tighter, still shaking slightly. With her paws over her face, she sobbed. They really had gone home without her!

CHAPTER SEVEN
Emu, the Cat

"Now what could make a cute little kitty cat like you be a sobbin'?" The voice was gruff, raspy, and positively dripping with false sugarcoated sympathy. Giggles instinctively knew this was a voice not to be trusted. Startled, Giggles leaped to her feet. Her tail straight up as her fur along her back instantly stood on end, she softly hissed. She'd hissed the same way on many occasions when Paisley had annoyed her, although it hadn't scared him, either.

"I'm right sorry, little girl. I didn't mean to scare ya none," the same gruff voice said, the false sympathy gone now, and in its place sarcastic amusement. Giggles sprung round facing him head on. He was a scruffy, mangy, ginger tomcat with broken whiskers, a half chewed off tail, and a knowing glint in his light yellow eyes. Giggles could smell his breath and see his chipped, dirty yellow, teeth as he talked. She backed away still further, her fear making it impossible to reply, "So ya want ta be a hedge cat, do ya?" he continued. "Well now, it's not for everyone, an' by the looks of ya, ya much too genteel—a young lady almost," he said with a lecherous glint in his eyes as he ran them slowly over her body and then back again. Although it was the lazy knowing drawl in his words and the way he dribbled as he spoke that scared Giggles the most.

"Well now, me lady, I's be Emu, Emu the hedge cat and I's happier to make your acquaintance than ya can ever imagine!" he said, still dribbling and moving closer as he extended his dirty paw in her direction. Giggles moved back just as far as she could as she remembered the warning the owls had given her about Emu, the mangy hedge cat.

"Catch me if you can," a young, high-pitched voice suddenly called. She thought they must be two very small badgers as they raced past, although she'd never actually met one. Soon, two more quickly raced past. One almost knocked Giggles over, while the other ran headfirst into Emu, who was blocking their way. Giggles, remembered seeing pictures of badgers Suzy had shown her in one of her books. She thought these creatures must definitely be little badgers as they were flat and cuddly, with black and white stripes covering their faces. They looked very smartly dressed, Giggles thought, peeking at them while they raced by and then back again.

"I can easily catch you; there, tagged you! Catch me if you can!" called another equally young voice. The young badger cubs ran fast around and around the tree trunk. Each time, they knocked into Emu, pretending he wasn't there. They continued laughing and teasing each other. It was a delightful, fast-paced, and furious game, and to Giggles, it looked like huge fun.

"Alright, you lot. Now settle down this instant," a kindly older male voice instructed. From around the other side of the tree trunk, two large badgers appeared. They, too, were smartly dressed in grayish fur coats and white stripes over their slightly pointed, kindly faces.

"Oh dear! Goodness me, miss, I do apologize. I don't think my energetic brood saw you there," said Mr. Badger. He stopped and stared at Giggles before tipping a paw to his forehead in her direction. Moments later, the four rascally cubs came to a fast halt, sandwiching into each other before also staring at Giggles. Finally, Mrs. Badger introduced herself and her family.

"I'm so sorry we frightened you," she began.

"We thought you needed rescuing, actually," added one of the little badgers.

"Quiet, Lester! Do let your mother get a word in and introduce us to the stranger," Mr. Badger said.

"Sorry, Mummy," Lester added. He looked at the ground kicking dirt with his rear paw as he spoke.

"Well now. How nice it is to get a newcomer in our part of the hedge. I'm Bilby Badger, and this is my husband, Burgundy. No doubt, you've met our brood of unruly young cubs. This is Moo, Boo, Buky, and of course, Lester."

"Hello, I'm Giggles," Giggles answered. She was beginning to feel very uncomfortable, although it was not due to the Badger family. She felt rather like she was sitting on lots of Mummy's knitting needles, but there was nowhere else to go. The small space surrounding her was completely full of badgers.

"Oh yes, and you're a hedge cat, of course—and, may I say, a definite improvement over that mangy, good-for-nothing Emu," Burgundy Badger added.

"Why thank you," Giggles said, "but I'm not really a hedge cat, and I really don't want to be one. You see, I'm . . . " Giggles was about to tell them she was lost, but again Lester butted in before she could finish.

"Mummy, Daddy, why is she not facing Buky when she speaks? That's just not fair!"

"Oh, I'm sorry," Giggles began as Lester again interrupted her before Mrs. Badger stopped him.

"Lester, remember your manners," Bilby Badger administered as Boo added, "He just doesn't have any!"

"Quiet now," Burgundy said, as they all stopped talking and stared again at Giggles. "What my cub means," Burgundy said, "is that young Buky is deaf. He reads lips, so you have to face him when you speak, otherwise someone has to face him and tell him what you've just said. He's very young and is only just learning."

"I'm sorry. I didn't know," Giggles added.

"It's quite alright, my dear. We Badgers have the utmost patience with all our cubs, and we love him just as much as all the rest," Burgundy concluded.

Suddenly, a long, golden animal hurried toward them. Giggles stared, as its body was running very close to the ground and its slightly darker tail was bringing up the rear. Giggles moved backward as much as she could to avoid the strange looking animal; it reminded Giggles of the delicious long, golden, hot dogs Mummy sometimes cooked for Sunday tea. However, as she stared at the newcomer, she had no idea just what it was.

The area was now definitely over-crowded. Giggles was relieved to notice Emu had long since departed.

"Oh dear, oh dear me! I can't imagine where she's got to," came the voice of a second animal. Giggles couldn't see who the voice belong to, but she knew it was following closely behind the long, golden one.

Burgundy Badger laughed as his two weary friends hurriedly appeared. He quickly introduced them to Giggles. "These are my old friends, Willy Weasel, and the old chap behind him is Stoddard Stoat."

Willy Weasel nodded slightly and winked at Giggles. However, looking at his face Giggles quickly lost her appetite. Willy Weasel had a fierce-looking face and sharp teeth. He could never be my friend, Giggles decided, turning her attention to Stoddard Stoat. Stoddard Stoat had a kindly face and was smaller than Willy Weasel. He wore a dark brown coat with an attractive white underbelly. Perched snugly on his head was a small black cap. Giggles secretly admitted he was much cuter than Willy Weasel. Stoddard Stoat had a small round face, big eyes, and large, healthy, dark whiskers; she liked him even though he appeared somewhat nervous with an anxious disposition.

Burgundy continued, "Meet the new hedge cat, Giggles."

"Oh dear, oh dear me, why yes, yes, how nice, charmed I'm sure!" said Stoddard. "We're all looking for my wife, Silby Stoat. Can't find her anywhere! You haven't seen her by any chance, have you? Oh dear, oh dear me," the old Stoat said, still quite agitated. His whiskers twitched and his eyeglasses slipped from his small nose before Boo quickly retrieved them.

"Yes, yes, thank you, quite so, can't hope to find her without them," Stoddard said nervously, looking this way and that.

"You did see the foxes sniffing around earlier, I suppose. You see, she hasn't been seen since," Willy Weasel calmly added, again winking at Giggles.

"We'll all look for Mrs. Stoat. Can we, Daddy?" the four baby badgers asked in unison. Mr. and Mrs. Badger nodded their agreement. Then everyone seemed to race off disappearing in all directions.

Giggles stayed just where she was, feeling quite bewildered with all the new faces and activity and then being so quickly abandoned. She moved slightly as again she became aware of something very prickly underneath her. Again she wiggled, thinking perhaps she had sat on a blackberry bush.

"I didn't want you to sit on me, but I didn't want to frighten you, either," a very polite voice said from underneath her. Giggles leaped into the air, only to hit a large branch just above her head.

"Oh my, now I know I've frightened you. I'm really very sorry, Giggles."

"How did you know my name?"

"Why, you've been sitting on me for some time. And, may I say, your fur is rather hot and very heavy," said the gentle, deep voice. Giggles stared as a small, pointed, black snout soon uncurled from a ball of yellowish, white-tipped quills. His snout protruded from a white face and underbelly. To Giggles, his round black eyes and deep voice seemed kind. The remarkable creature soon wiped the sweat from its brow and continued slowly unrolling a mass of long, spiky, prickly quills.

"Have you seen my monocle, by any chance? Always manage to lose the jolly thing when I curl up so tightly," he said, looking around, before focusing again on Giggles.

CHAPTER EIGHT
Hedley Hedgehog to the Rescue

"Oh do forgive my bad manners, especially after you've sat on me for so very long and endured my spines. How do you do—I'm Hedley Hedgehog," he said, producing a rather small, soft, white paw from under his quills. Giggles liked him immediately and took his tiny paw in hers before shaking it briefly.

"It really is rather crowded under the hedge grove lately, don't you think?" Hedley asked, stretching himself to his full length.

"Well, I really don't know. I'm new here," Giggles replied, relaxing and settling down with her tail neatly wrapped around her in preparation for a cozy chat.

"Well now, Giggles, you see, most of these little animals have their main residences' deep in the foliage of the woods, and this is only their holiday home. I, on the other hand, have only one residence, lonely though it is. All year round I live entirely under the hedges, and I hog as much of the hedge as I can—hence the name hedgehog."

"Oh, here is your monocle, Mr. Hedley?" Giggles reached over and retrieved his eyeglass; it had become lodged in his back quills.

"Well thank you, my dear Giggles," he said, bowing low.

Before Giggles continued, "Oh, now I understand why it's so crowded under here, and just who you are."

"Exactly, Giggles. Most of these characters have to go out at times to get food, and that's scary for them. I don't need to go anywhere—but if I want to, it's not at all scary for me. Nothing can hurt me; I am a hedgehog and quite invincible!" Hedley said raising his paws in the air to emphasize his point. Giggles liked him a lot; he had laughter in his voice and a happy sparkle in his dark eyes. His speech also intrigued her; it was very proper and with an accent only a hedgehog could have.

"Oh, Hedley, you are funny. But I really don't think anyone's invincible. That's a very brave word indeed, Mr. Hedley."

"Why yes, Giggles, you see us hedgehogs are quite unique, I assure you. Did you know my ancestry goes back over fifteen million years? With age comes wisdom, and with adaption comes survival, you understand. We can go where we choose, and when danger threatens, we curl up tightly into a prickly ball. Should anyone or anything touch us, our sharp quills will immediately stick straight up and hurt our enemy. You didn't get hurt when you sat on me because I knew I liked you and didn't want to hurt you. I know it was still rather uncomfortable as you kept squirming," he said, sounding very grand.

"Oh, I see, and thank you for not really hurting me, although your quills are very sharp."

"Yes, they are, and I like to keep them that way. It is certainly better to be my friend than my enemy, Giggles," he said kindly.

"Why are you lonely, Hedley? Don't you play with the other hedgehogs?" Giggles asked, curious now.

"Why, Giggles can't you see I'm an old gentleman hedgehog? And that my playing days are long over?" he answered. Giggles quickly nodded, not wanting to offend him. "Well, I'm lonely because my beautiful wife, Bonne, left me. I'm very sad. I still love her very much, and when you really love someone, you can't just stop loving them because they no longer share your feelings. Without someone to care about and love you, you're just not a real hedgehog and never can be. That's why I'm sad and lonely."

"Oh, I am sorry she left you, it does sound lonely. Maybe she'll come home soon," Giggles added.

"I doubt it. You see, Bonne is a very beautiful hedgehog, with the longest, shiniest spines, the darkest eyes, and the whitest fur you've ever seen." A tear escaped the corner of his eye and he quickly mopped it up with his paw.

"But you sound as though you still love her very much."

"Oh yes, I do, and I always will. But she found herself a younger hedgehog, and I think he must be more fun. Also, I think he can probably roll down hills faster than me, and maybe, just maybe, he's a better dancer. Our son, Huckleberry, is more confused and hurt than I am. I have explained to him many times how it isn't his fault. I told him repeatedly that what happens in a marriage is between a husband and wife; it has nothing to do with the children and never stops parents from loving them."

"Then I guess it's true," added Giggles, trying to give Hedley time to compose himself as another solitary tear ran down his furry cheek before dripping off the end of his dark nose.

"Giggles, now that I no longer feel loved, I am no longer a real, worthwhile hedgehog," he said. Again, a tear escaped the corner of his eye; again, he quickly used his paw to wipe it away.

"I am sorry for you, Mr. Hedley," Giggles added, not knowing what else to say to a happy hedgehog that now seemed so sad.

"Well, Giggles, it was my fault, really. You see, Bonne said I had trust issues. You do know what trust is, don't you?" he paused to ask. Giggles nodded, vaguely remembering the owls asking her the same question, even though she couldn't really remember all of the answer. She didn't want to actually say yes in case it was a lie. She was not sure of the full meaning of trust, but she was very sure lying was wrong.

"Well, maybe I didn't trust her as much as she would have liked. She was young, fun, and very pretty. Anyway, in the end I guess my lack of trust drove her away. You see, Giggles, trust is a funny thing; you need to receive it as part of feeling loved. You also need to understand it enough to feel comfortable giving it back. Then, of course, with trust comes responsibility. It's all about giving and receiving what's important to one another. You can never completely trust anyone you don't really know. I often ask myself, just how do you really know someone? It is a huge part of friendship, after all! Without trust, there can be no love, but without love, there can still be trust. You do know about friendship, trust, and love, don't you, Giggles?" Hedley asked, looking at her intently.

"Yes, of course. Well, I think I do," Giggles finished, knowing it sounded lame but she was now feeling confused and rather unsure about many things. What Giggles did know was that Hedley was one very smart hedgehog. She knew she was learning some very grown up and important things.

"Love is about giving without ever expecting anything in return. It's something you give because you want to, not because you have to."

"But I think everyone wants love," Giggles said, a little confused now as she realized Hedley's thinking was much too intelligent for her.

"You see, Giggles, if you haven't known love, you can't miss it; but once you've had it, you want it always, and you need it desperately," he said, still rather upset. His words upset Giggles too, and before she knew it, she was sobbing and telling Hedley her sad story. She was almost finished when little Lester Badger came bounding into their space and abruptly interrupted their conversation.

"Oh, you're Giggles, aren't you?" he said breathlessly. "It's almost dark now, and the owls are waiting to speak to you. Hurry, hurry! This way!" He said racing off again. Giggles looked at Hedley before he quickly reassured her,

"Go quickly, Giggles. The owls are wise, and you are very fortunate they want to speak to you. Maybe they will help. Go now, little Giggles, as fast as you can. I will follow to make sure all is well."

Quickly Giggles raced after the little badger cub before Hedley

Hedgehog had even finished his sentence. She had to push her way through the sharp, dry twigs; Lester was much smaller than she was and needed less space. He kept stopping and turning around to tell her to hurry—the owls wouldn't wait. As she emerged from the gloom of the hedge, Giggles was amazed to see it was already getting dark.

"Whoooooooo, whooooooooo! There she is, Alfie. See along further. I can just see her white head peeking out from the hedge," Ollie said. The two large owls tried to speak to her as they flew above, blocking the moonlight. However, even when she came all the way out from under the hedge she couldn't hear everything they were saying.

"Never mind, Giggles! Just come down the hill, and we'll take you ... whoooo whooo" This was all she heard as they flew by again. By now Giggles was completely out in the open and moving down the small hill. It felt good after the confines of the hedge. She breathed deeply several times until suddenly, the silence was shattered by loud, deep barking. It didn't sound far away.

CHAPTER NINE
Giggles, the Flying Cat

Giggles stopped, terrified. It was Sam, that smelly, black dog again, except this time he was bounding fast in her direction. He must have been sleeping in the barn, Giggles quickly thought. She had never been this side of the hedge before and now realized it was a barnyard.

"Run, Giggles! Quickly, run as fast as you can!" Ollie's voice called urgently from above. "Oh dear Alfie, he's gaining on her . . . oh no . . . who whooooo, whoooooooooooo!"

Giggles ran faster than she had ever run in her life. It felt almost like she was flying. The barking was very close now; she could even feel the dog's hot breath on her tail. Then she stopped deadly still. Suddenly, from out of nowhere, the big, black, smelly dog was in front of her, barking wildly, his back feet still while his front paws jumped from side to side. Giggles didn't know what to do or where to go!

"Alfie, I'm going to dive for her . . . whoooooooooooo," Ollie called from somewhere close by.

"No, Ollie, no, it's much too dangerous!"

The dog continued barking, and then, abruptly, the barking

stopped. For a few seconds there was silence. Giggles stayed exactly where she was, and all was still, until suddenly Sam let out a small howl. The next thing Giggles felt was Ollie's strong feet about her, lifting her swiftly off the ground as she carried her high into the air. For a second, her surprise overtook her fear. From high above the hedge, she looked down into the barnyard to see Sam the dog, backing away from Hedley, who had rolled into a tight, round ball, his quills sticking out in all directions. He looked very prickly and quite dangerous. Hedley had rolled down the small hill and right into Sam. He'd let out a loud howl as the sharp prickles stuck into his soft fleshy nose. Oh, Hedley, Giggles thought you are indeed a true gentleman and dear friend.

Very gently, Ollie flew over Alfie and let Giggles fall from her feet right onto Alfie's soft, light brown, back feathers. Giggles held on tight as the wind pinned her ears and whiskers back against her head. Giggles almost purred as she realized this time she really was flying!

"Giggles, I know you're frightened, but you don't need to hold quite so tightly. Trust me, I am an expert flyer and will give you a very soft ride," Alfie whispered.

"Oh, Alfie, I'm sorry! I do trust you. I have just learned a lot about trust. And yes, it is a very soft ride indeed, but still quite scary for a young house cat like myself. I don't believe cat's usually fly," she answered as Ollie flew close.

"Giggles, did you hear what we said to you when you were on the ground?"

"Only that you were going to take me somewhere."

"That was just a little piece of it. You see, early this morning, as the sun began to rise and before we put our heads under our wings, Alfie flew through the village. Giggles there are '*lost*' posters of you everywhere. They all have your photo on them, and so we knew it was you. He spoke to some of his friends, and they said little Suzy has been asking for you and searching for you every single day . . ."

Ollie was still speaking as Giggles said, "Oh really! Then, Suzy really does love me!" Giggles exclaimed.

"'Oh yes, Giggles, I would say she loves you very much. Whooooooooo!"

"She came to the barnyard and was calling for me," Giggles said.

"Well why didn't you go to her? Do you really want to become a hedge cat, like Emu? Whooooooooooooo!" Alfie asked.

"Of course not! It was the foxes. They were sniffing and yapping loudly, and if Suzy and Daddy hadn't turned up just when they did, the foxes would have eaten me. Those foxes are very aggressive and persistent, just like you told me."

"Whooooooooooo! Dear me, you were very lucky Giggles. Very lucky indeed," Alfie said as Ollie continued, "Well, we're almost there," Ollie said. "We're leaving you at a hedge close to the village. You'll be able to see Suzy when she comes around. This time, run to her, Giggles, run to her! She won't keep searching forever. I know she has already been absent for several days from school, and I hear the school will soon notify her parents. They think Suzy has only taken one day off from school, but soon they'll find out she has taken more. Lying is very bad, and it doesn't excuse her even if she did it for you, Giggles. She may fall behind in her lessons, and it will be your fault." Giggles felt guilty at Ollie's words, but before she could answer, they neared the ground. Giggles could have flown much longer, but all too soon it was over. It was a very smooth landing, just as Alfie had promised.

"The hedge is over there, Giggles. Hide in it until morning and then watch and wait for Suzy to arrive. Good luck, little hedge cat," Alfie said.

"Oh, thank you very much for being so kind. I knew you were kind from the very first," Giggles said.

"Look out for us in your garden. We will find out where you live, and when you hear whoooooooo, whoooooooooooo, you'll know who," Alfie said as they started to fly away.

"I will, I will, and thank you!" Giggles said again as the two large owls silently disappeared into the night. As Giggles stood beside the hedge, they circled over her. Into the darkness Ollie's gentle voice said, "Giggles watch for us and, Giggles, yes, we will be your friends." Then as Giggles stared up into the darkness, they disappeared for the last time. She didn't move for some time, but stood looking up at the night sky until she became aware of all the strange night noises surrounding her.

CHAPTER TEN
Paisley Serenades Giggles

The new hedge wasn't nearly as thick, and Giggles moved swiftly into what she thought was the thickest part. She was careful not to disturb any bunnies or nesting hedge birds. She was tired and hungry and she just wanted a place to sleep. Her front paws slipped slightly on a snail trail, and she followed it a few inches to the snail—a tasty treat. She was just about to crunch the shell loudly when she heard a faint sobbing coming from somewhere close by. Giggles curiosity almost got the better of her, although she could no longer manage to stifle a yawn. She would investigate later—all she wanted to do now was sleep. However, the sobbing continued, until Giggles realized someone must be hurt or in need of a friend.

As she moved toward the sobbing, it stopped. She stood very still until a slight movement in the gloom up ahead caught her attention. Looking closer, she could just make out the shape of a hedgehog, but it wasn't Hedley—he was much bigger.

"Hello, hedgehog, are you alright?" Giggles asked, tentatively moving closer.

"Oh dear me, no, but I will be. I know I shouldn't cry. It really is my own fault, but I've made some very silly mistakes in my life. Sorry, how rude of me—I'm Bonne." The delicate little hedgehog wiped her eyes before extending her paw toward Giggles.

"Hello, I'm Giggles. I know what you mean about silly choices. I've made some too," Giggles said, trying to make the young hedgehog feel comfortable. At that moment, Giggles suddenly realized who Bonne was.

"Oh, really? I guess you must have. You don't look much like a hedge cat. I've never seen a green cat before—why your fur almost matches your eyes. I think you made a bad choice wanting to be a hedge cat," Bonne said, still looking rather sad.

"Well, Bonne, I never wanted to be a hedge cat. I had a home I loved and people who really loved me and I loved them. I was very happy."

"So why are you here?" Bonne asked. Her sobbing slowed, and she appeared slightly more interested.

"Well, I was very silly. I was bored one afternoon and wanted some fun, so I chased two very beautiful, blue, butterflies. On and on I ran. It was exciting—the pretty butterflies, the freedom, everything—until I reached the woods and realized I didn't know where I was. I was far from home. Far away from everything and everyone I loved. I'd left it all behind for a little excitement and two silly butterflies—butterflies I could never catch; they'd always be just out of reach. They never cared about me at all. They were just playing games and teasing me. They had their fun then flew off and left me alone, scared and very lost, far away from my home and the family I loved," Giggles said as a tear escaped her eye and ran down her fluffy face, onto the end of her nose.

"Giggles, I understand more than you can ever know. I did the same thing. I went after a little excitement and left behind the one hedgehog that truly cared and loved me. He wasn't the most exciting chap all the time, but he was a kind, considerate, caring gentleman, and he loved me no matter what, all the time. We were happy, you see. I just didn't realize how very happy we were. Now it's all too late," Bonne Hedgehog said as another sob escaped her.

"But why is it too late, Bonne? Are you married to another?"

"That's a very personal question, Giggles," Bonne said kindly.

"Oh, I'm sorry. It really isn't any of my business," Giggles quickly added, yawning uncontrollably again.

"It's okay. I was for a very short time, but that ended ages ago. He didn't really care for me. He just wanted to have fun too, and when the fun stopped, he left. He turned out to be just like your butterflies, he never cared about me, either," Bonne said in a very small voice, looking at the ground as she spoke.

"So, why don't you go back to the one you love and who loves you?" Giggles asked, thinking it may also be too personal.

"I can't. I already left him. He was a good hedgehog, one of the best. I wish I could go back. But I have my pride, you know," Bonne said. For several moments Giggles didn't answer as she tried to think of the right words to express what was on her mind.

"Well, I think you can easily keep your pride intact and stay alone. But I wonder, just maybe, wouldn't you rather swallow your pride and chase your happiness? Otherwise you'll be sad always and have to live with your regrets and loneliness forever." Giggles asked, feeling very proud of herself for giving such a clever, grown-up answer. She felt Hedley would have given much the same sort of intelligent answer. She hoped Bonne would think about it and go to Hedley.

Bonne didn't answer. Giggles waited and waited very patiently for her to say something. She was obviously deep in thought. Giggles yawned some more, and waited before she decided to nap a little while she waited for Bonne's answer.

She curled up tightly into a fuzzy, pale green ball and slept. She dreamed of butterflies, Suzy, her food bowl, Mummy and Daddy, and even Hedley and Bonne Hedgehog. It would have been a great dream if she hadn't kept hearing that confounded Paisley singing.

When she awoke, she realized it wasn't Paisley at all—but it was indeed singing. Dawn had broken, and the early birds were greeting the new day, each competing with the other singing their loudest and best early morning songs.

In front of Giggles, scratched in the dusty earth, was a message from Bonne:

"Sleep tight, little friend. I am going home. Hope you will also. Bonne."

There was no time to stretch this morning. As a voice behind Giggles said quickly, "Oh my, you frightened me! What are you, and why are you under my hedge? Leave at once!" The voice was speaking very fast. Giggles searched the depths of the hedge before finding the origin of the voice. It belonged to a long, skinny animal that was very close to the ground. It had a pointed nose and beady black eyes.

"Oh pardon me, I'm a house cat. What are you?" Giggles asked, trying not to appear as frightened as she felt.

"A what cat?" Oh, a hedge cat, you say. Well, not under my hedge, you're not," he replied rather indignantly.

"So what are you?" Giggles asked, trying to take his mind off his anger. She hoped he'd forget about throwing her out.

"It's really none of your business, but I'm Freddy Ferret, and this is my hedge. Always has been and always will be. Emu's not welcome here either—nasty, dirty creature that he is—and neither are you. I expect that you're friends, as you certainly don't look like relatives. Anyway, you probably have some mean, nasty plan in store for me. I don't like mean and nasty, but if I have to, I can be quite mean and nasty myself. Do you understand me?" Freddy had a small pink nose; brown whiskers that curled downward at the ends; small, round, pink ears; and a white face. Freddy Ferret definitely looked kinder than he sounded.

"I'm no friend of Emu's, and I'm just going to be here a very short time. So please . . ." Giggles never finished her sentence as the long, slinking form of the old, mangy, ginger tomcat pushed its way into the hedge.

"Well now, if it ain't me girlfriend Giggles, how charming, how charming indeed," Emu drooled as he moved closer, much too close for Giggles liking. She backed away just as far as she could. Even though she felt sharp twigs poking into her skin through her thick fur, she continued to back away. Emu's breath smelled rancid this morning, and more tufts of his fur were missing. The very sight of him made an involuntary shiver ripple over Giggles fur.

"Well, I'll be leaving you two old friends to chat then. But don't linger too long under my hedge," Freddy Ferret warned, making a hasty retreat as Emu growled and hissed, before chasing the frightened ferret for a short distance and then returning. Giggles knew she should have taken that opportunity to run, but Emu was only gone a few seconds, and she was petrified. He had a huge dribbling problem, and he positively drooled as he spoke to Giggles. She slowly backed away as he moved toward her.

"Well now, my sweet little kitty. This is a very advantageous meetin'! I's been thinkin' bout you. In fact, you're all I's been thinkin' about." Giggles felt really frightened now and was having trouble moving any farther backwards.

"I's been sniffin' out ya sweet scent this morning at the wrong hedge, by the looks of it. But all's well. I's found ya, and I's never lettin' ya out of me sight again, little kitty," he said. He began lowering his body into a pounce, wiggling his rear as his chewed-off tail flicked to and fro, to and fro.

Suddenly, a voice came from under Giggles's rear, followed by the worst odor she had ever smelled. "Why did you have to sit on me?" the voice said, "I've done nothing to you!" Just at the moment Giggles saw Emu was about to pounce, she shot past him, propelled mainly by fear but also by the horrid smell. She raced out of the hedge with Emu in hot pursuit. Somewhere, a dog barked. The barking was rapidly getting closer—and so was Emu.

"Ya be a frisky one! Never mind. Old Emu can catch the best of them, and I's always enjoys a good chase," he said, almost upon her. To her right she could see a large, brown dog barking and racing straight for her, his leash dragging in the mud.

"Giggles, oh, Giggles! Over here, quickly! Run fast, Giggles, run!" Giggles couldn't believe her ears. It was Suzy's voice—but where was she?

"Giggles, hurry, run! Over here, Giggles, hurry!" Giggles looked slightly to her left and there was Suzy, holding open the rear car door and encouraging her to hurry. Just the sight of her was all the inspiration Giggles needed. From somewhere deep inside, she found the extra strength, power, and courage she needed to run still faster, but as she did so she felt Emu swatting at her tail. The dog was almost upon her too.

"Quick, Giggles! Leap into the car!" Suzy screamed, quickly closing the door. They heard a loud thud as Emu hit the closed car door. Hissing and barking followed; then a loud yelp rose up as Emu obviously scratched the dog's nose. That was all Giggles remembered. Suzy held her tightly in her arms, kissing and hugging her.

"What is that dreadful smell? Oh, Giggles, it smells like you've befriended a skunk," Daddy said as he wound down the window.

"Oh Daddy, Mummy just won't believe this!" Suzy shouted. "Giggles, we've looked and looked for you everywhere. We've all called and called you. Mummy lost her voice yesterday evening from calling."

"Oh yes, she really did, Giggles," Daddy agreed before he added, "Well, young Giggles, I know cats don't like baths, but you're going home to have one if you're going to be our Giggles, the house cat, again!"

"Yes, you are, Giggles. Why, your fur's all green, too!"

"It's okay. I really don't mind. I'll do anything just to stay home forever," Giggles answered in a tiny, frightened voice. She was trying to catch her breath and quiet her racing heart.

"But why did you run away? Don't you know we love you so very much? What did we do, Giggles? Please, oh please tell us, and we promise we'll never do it again," Suzy begged.

"Giggles, I guess it was Grandma's birthday party," Daddy apologized. "We're so sorry we didn't take you. No one's slept a wink since we thought we'd lost you forever," Daddy added, switching off the engine in the driveway to the cottage. As he turned around to stroke Giggles, he added, "You're right, Suzy. She is green, as well as smelly. I'll ask Mummy to quickly fill the little tub with warm, soapy water, and you can take her straight around to the back garden."

Suzy couldn't stop hugging Giggles, and for the first time in several days, Giggles found her purr. At first, it was just a small purr, but soon it became long, deep, and very, very happy!

Mummy, Daddy, and Suzy bathed Giggles in the sunshine. They kept apologizing for having to bathe her, but Giggles just kept purring. She didn't mind one little bit, although after her bath she knew that no self-respecting cat would dare look in the mirror. Mummy gave Giggles a warm air-dry with her hair dryer. They all laughed when Giggles emerged larger, whiter, and fluffier than ever. They said she looked like a round, white, ball of fluff with bright green eyes.

"It's not breakfast or dinnertime, Giggles, but your food bowl is full of your favorite treats, and your milk dish too," Mummy added.

Giggles was now clean and dry and didn't need to be told twice. She raced through the house, and before the others arrived, she was hungrily licking up the last of her food. Suzy scooped her up into her arms again as together they stood around stroking her; they stroked her back, under her chin, and her belly. Giggles purred so much her eyes closed with pleasure.

She awoke sometime later on the end of Suzy's bed. Suzy lay close by, cuddling her and reading. She'd never been allowed to sleep on Suzy's bed in the daytime. Neither was she allowed to sleep there during the night, but she often did, just until Suzy went to sleep.

As Giggles yawned happily and stretched out to her full length, as only a cat can do, she realized something was missing. She listened— yes, something was definitely missing. She wiggled free from Suzy's arms and lazily strolled into the living room. Perhaps her dearest wish was finally answered. Had they actually realized she was all they needed? Was Paisley finally gone?

As she looked up toward the cage, a very loud song broke forth. It pierced the silence and Giggles's dreams; it was much louder than she remembered. Looking up into the cage, Giggles green eyes opened wide with horror. She stared into the cage in disbelief. She blinked several times before she looked into the cage again. She didn't want to believe her eyes; maybe it was just a bad joke. But, no, what she saw sitting side by side on the perch, was not one canary, but two.

"Hi, Giggles! Thought you were never coming home; really wished you weren't, actually. Meet Plaid, Giggles. Plaid was Grandma's canary, but now he's mine." Paisley said, puffing his chest out with pride before continuing. "Plaid, this is the cat I've been telling you about."

"Oh yes! She's the one we composed the song for then, Paisley. Hello, Giggles," Plaid said, sounding far less arrogant then Paisley. Giggles couldn't respond. Her worst nightmare loomed menacingly in that cage—and now there were two!

Giggles stood very still and thought; she thought about horrible Emu, she thought about the wise owls, she thought about all that Hedley had told her, and she thought about Buky Badger, who was deaf. Giggles knew he, for one, would have given anything to be able to hear Paisley's songs. Then Giggles thought about Suzy, the cottage, and all the things she loved. Finally, she thought about Paisley and his new friend who, together, had composed a song just for her. She stood very still for a few moments longer and gazed around the small, shabby room. She looked at the worn-out rug, the fire that hadn't yet been lit, and the general clutter all around her. Giggles knew for certain these were all the things she loved, and all the people she loved most in the whole world. However, it was mainly about the people who loved her. Giggles knew without a doubt she was a very loved and real cat. Yes, she was a very real cat, indeed!

She looked up at the two small, yellow birds sitting side by side as they sat looking down at her from their perch inside the cage.

"So, Giggles, do you like our song? We named it after you," Plaid said as Paisley continued, "Yes, Giggles, we named it the 'Giggles Serenade,'" Paisley replied proudly, puffing out his small yellow chest.

Giggles stood still a little longer. Finally, she realized that even though you might not love everything in your life, if they love you enough, you should be able to accept them for who they are. You should take what they offer and receive it in the spirit in which it is given, even if you don't always want it. It seldom hurts to give a little in return.

Giggles continued purring loudly, as looking up into the cage at the two little yellow birds, she finally replied, "Paisley, Plaid, I like it very much, very much indeed." As she watched, the two little birds seem to grow with pride and pleasure at her words, and so Giggles added, "Actually, I'd love to hear it again."

. . . And together, they all lived happily ever after . . .

The End